WHIPPOORWILL WILLINGLY

Whippoorwill Willingly

Margaret Dulaney

Listen Well Publishing

WHIPPOORWILL WILLINGLY

1

I F YOU knew my mother, you wouldn't be surprised to learn that she signed us up for something called the International Conference on Animal Communication. The added enticement that the gathering was to take place in a small village in Switzerland, in the canton of Ticino, nestled in the foothills of the Alps (which, if you could see these hills, look suspiciously like their larger cousins), was simply too much for my romantic parent. The combination of mountains, the Italian language (Ticino is located in the Italian-speaking section of Switzerland), and the exploration of the mysterious thoughts of our brothers and sisters in fur and feathers was so deliciously inviting that we found ourselves, one mid-August night, flying across the Atlantic from our home in New York City to join in the revelry.

The details of my time in Ticino have remained as if freshly experienced. And, though I tell this story from the distance of well over a decade, my memories stand in sharp contrast to the years that came before. In many ways this was to be the beginning of my life's journey, signaling a life's worth of friendship and guidance.

Arriving on a Sunday, we checked into a charming hotel at the edge of a tidy little village and began the very next morning to attend the various talks and workshops. I will report, with no intentional disrespect to our presenters (whom I am sure were all very enthusiastic about their subjects), that there was not a single animal present, other than the human variety. And although, as I feel obliged to repeat, the speakers themselves were quite engaging, by the second day I had grown just a smidgeon restless. Or perhaps I should say, I was eager to experience an actual heart-to-heart connection with a creature of any variety other than the human. But then animals have always held the power to both fascinate and comfort me. Animals are completely devoid of criticism or judgement. I wonder if you have noticed this, dear reader? They might flinch and hide from a human who has been erratic or unkind to them, but they would never judge them as we do one another in the world of people. I will leave this subject for now but promise to return to it further along in my story.

It was in the late morning hours of the second day of the conference when I found myself alone and seated in the auditorium. There was a break in the program, and the audience members had moved outside to stretch their legs, or perhaps, as I suspected, to attempt to catch a glimpse of some solid sample of the animal kingdom (a bird or two, for example). And, though tempted myself to breathe a bit of fresh air, I had opted to keep my seat and ponder a bit on the merits of the last talk.

After a moment, a man entered the hall and sat two seats away from me. I presumed he did so in anticipation of the next presentation. We sat for a bit in silence. Or at least I was silent. The man was wordless but up to a good deal of rustlings with his program and fidgetings over his comfort. Eventually, he turned to me.

"And what brings you to be at this conference, my dear?"

You might wince at the intimacy of this question. I might have done so as well, had I not turned to look at the man. Such a kindness shone on his round face, with its pleasingly bright expression. He wore a comfortable smile, as if I were the very person he had wished to see at that moment. Indeed, he seemed so familiar with me that I thought I must have met him at some point in the past few days. *Maybe*, I thought, *he has helped me or my mother in some way: carried our luggage, opened a door.* I hoped we had been sufficiently gracious if he had offered us help. We had grown like an old married couple, my mother and I, often unaware of those around us.

"Well," I answered, careful to make up for my not knowing who he was, "I do love animals, all animals. I have made a very careful study of the squirrels of Central Park, in New York City, filling whole notebooks of observations. I find the life of animals endlessly fascinating, and I thought I might learn something that I hadn't known or dreamed of before. I hope to be enlightened in some way, surprised even."

"Oh, oh dear," the man responded. He looked a

bit pained over my expectations and my inevitable disappointment. "Dear me."

"In truth it was my mother who signed us both up, only weeks ago." I continued, "Do you know my mother?" I felt sure he must know her, for he seemed more and more known to me. "Her name is Louise, and she is quite stunning, though she hasn't a hint of how she effects people. I wonder whether you might have at least seen her. She walks around under a great pile of hair, dresses in green, always, and wears shoes that the Elvin people might covet."

The man raised the back of his hand to his mouth and softly cleared his throat. "I believe I might know who you are referring to, yes," saying so with a slightly suppressed grin, which subtlety I took to be a compliment to my mother.

"Were you interested in what the last speaker reported on her communications with the zebras?" I asked, changing the subject.

"Not in the least, no." He answered without hesitation or any ill will toward the woman whose presentation had just ended; his smile remained. "Were you?" he added.

"Faintly. I believe there was something she mentioned that might have had some real truth to it, something about the animal's love of being noticed. Perhaps we all love to be noticed? The stickiness is, in my view, that this is a talk in words about having a conversation with an animal, a creature that requires no words to communicate."

"An astute observation," agreed my companion.

"I would rather have a direct communication with the zebra, wouldn't you?"

"Without a doubt."

"Hm," I said. "Do you think it a bit odd that my mother and I chose to fly a third of the way around the world to attend a conference on animal communication when we might have been much more enlightened by driving just a few hours outside the island of Manhattan in the state of New York where we live, to visit a local farm?"

"Well," the man answered, again clearing his throat, but not saying anymore.

"Or do you think it unusual that someone like me would travel to Switzerland to attend a conference at all?"

The man stared forward, coughed slightly again into his fist, and seemed to go blank.

"Why, because I'm an eleven-year-old?"

I turned to him to study his honest face.

"Well, I must admit I was a bit surprised…" he stammered, wearing a bemused smile. "I was expecting…someone…well…"

"Expecting?"

"Did I say…?" He trailed off and looked genuinely startled at his choice of words. "Oh, dear…" He held his throat as if his voice box might have been taken hostage.

At which point I thought I should relieve his uneasiness by continuing to talk. I did this as a child and still do this, to comfort certain grownups. They can be so awkward. And so I powered forward.

"You would think that I would know better than to listen to a handful of people speaking for an earth full of creatures: beasts and birds and reptiles, each individual more complex and varied than all of the words expressed for the past two days could begin to convey and whose physical presence would speak more in half an hour." I took a moment to breathe. "Take squirrels, for instance. Each individual has her own singular characteristics. Fascinating. I wonder if one could make a living at squirrel observation? I'd like to contribute to the family piggybank, if you know what I mean, it's been me and Louise since I arrived on this planet and I'd like to add something to the… well, let's call it the squirrely bank." I laughed at my own joke and plowed on. "Honestly, my mother needed an outing, she is such a journeyman, you know, loves to travel and, of course, this is Switzerland."

I turned to the gentle man to see if he was beginning to settle. I found him hand on his chin, in deep thought, as if he would like to say something but hadn't quite arrived at the moment of being able to do so. I thought it best to forge on and give him a little more time.

"Louise, my mother Louise, signed up for a private session this afternoon with a woman from Minnesota who claims to have a psychic cat, or rather a cat that she asserts has the power to see into the future."

"Ah," answered the man, still looking a bit distracted.

"I have a cat," I told him.

"Tinkerbell," returned my companion, still staring at the back of the seat in front of him.

I looked at the man, my jaw in my lap. Really, this was growing more and more mysterious. How on earth did the man know the name of my cat?

As my head turned toward him, his own plunged itself into his program, suddenly, seemingly, madly engrossed in the day's schedule. "Oh yes, here she is, yes, the woman whose domestic feline can see into the future."

I felt for the man, looking so keenly uncomfortable, so I decided to continue with my chitter-chattering.

"Though any cat, in my view, who can tear herself away from the present where she is utterly content and force herself into the future, where anything might happen, is a rare specimen indeed." I peeked over at the man. Nope, I concluded, still not ready to speak. I continued, "Actually, my cat left the world several months ago, and I'm having a tough time using the past tense when I speak of her."

"Oh, there's no need to do that," he answered.

I looked at him again, and again he buried himself in his program. "It says here that the feline will not be in attendance during the readings but will communicate telepathically from her home in…"

"Duluth. Duluth, Minnesota," I offered, and continued, "Yes, I spoke to this woman whose cat, due to quarantine restrictions, had opted to stay home. He is being looked after by a neighbor's child and naps between predictions, poor dear. Really, what people expect of their animals. Now Tinkerbell…" I paused to look over at my new friend to see if he was ready to explain how he could possibly be in possession of my cat's name, but he remained absorbed in his program, and therefore I continued to prattle on. "Tinkerbell is—oh, dear, you see, there I go with the present tense. Tinkerbell has never bothered with anything but the present moment, and this is one of the reasons that I find it almost absurd to refer to her in the past. This is also my reason for not trusting any cat who professes to see into the future. Though of course the cat is not claiming this, is he? It is the owner of the cat who…"

I could see that my new friend was beginning to be hypnotized by the number of words escaping from my mouth. *Good*, I thought, *he's calming*. "Some people think," I resumed, "that their cats wake them up at an unreasonable hour to be fed, but I see this very differently. I believe that they wake us at dawn, or just before dawn, because another beautiful day on earth has just announced itself, and they don't want us to miss it. My cat takes her main meal in the evening like all civilized creatures." I turned to my new friend to check on him. "You're looking at me again as if you are slightly confused. Is it really my age that is confounding you? Conferences are for grownups? That sort of thing?"

"I wouldn't describe this conference," the man answered with a stifled chuckle, "as being particularly adult-centric."

"Hmm," I murmured in agreement. "Tell me," I asked, "why did you decide to attend this conference?"

"Well, now we've come round to it." The man cleared his throat, sniffed, leaned in a bit toward me and down, as he was quite a tall man, and spoke in a quiet, confidential tone. "You are Whippoorwill Willingly, are you not?"

"Yes, that would be me," I answered and waited for him to go on. Apparently, his mind was on pause again, as he stared at a spot on the floor next to his shoe. This, of course, called for more filler.

"Yes, my mother named me Whippoorwill

because I kept her up at night with my singing during my formative years." I nattered on, "And yes, my family name is Willingly. I have always presumed that they inherited the surname because they are, all of them, willing to travel anywhere, at a moment's notice."

The man turned to me to take in this information, and his face brightened as if I had given him a rare and surprising gift. "I have a message for you."

"For me?"

"Yes, you are to travel."

"Travel?"

"Yes, by train, and I am to give you specific instructions."

"Instructions? Are they written down? Is there a pamphlet? I respond well to pamphlets."

"I must make a note of that for the future. But for today, however," the man explained, "I am to deliver these instructions by word of mouth." He added, "Don't worry, they are quite simple to follow."

"I can't imagine why I should travel. I am traveling. Does my mother know of this?"

"Your mother has been informed that you will be spending a few days away, yes, and is making arrangements to spend a little more time in the area to wait for your return."

"Days? Away from my mother? But how could you have convinced her of this?"

"There are times when a bit of fairy dust is called for," he said, with a slightly impish grin.

"You didn't tempt her with a retreat, did you? Louise cannot pass up a retreat center—mindfulness, yoga, meditation, she's a sucker for retreats."

"Precisely. She will be well taken care of," he offered with a comforting smile.

"You wouldn't happen to have a husband up that sleeve of yours, while you're at it, would you?"

"A husband?" the man questioned.

"I'm just kidding. I was thinking of your fairy dust."

The man chuckled, "I'll do what I can."

"It isn't that Louise is exactly looking for a husband, but I worry about her."

"We'll see what we can do." He smiled.

"Well, now that we have established where my mother will spend her days, would you mind telling me where I'm meant to be going?" I asked, a bit like a schoolteacher to a scattered child.

"Hmm…" the nice man mumbled. Adjusting

himself in his seat, he took a moment to think, cocking his head slightly to the left. And, after a moment or two, as if some invisible assistant had spoken an encouraging word into his ear, he answered, "Ah." And then, turning to me, he announced, "The Bright Ones are here."

"The Bright Ones?" I asked. But, before he could answer, something extraordinary seemed to happen inside of me. As if a door in my mind had opened, I was given a sharply vivid memory. I turned to the man, keenly alert. "I had a dream last night," I began. Staring off toward the ceiling, I recalled images in sharp snapshots.

"Of course, you did, yes," encouraged my companion.

"You know about the dream?" I turned to him, expectant.

"Well, no, but…" he caught himself, "continue, please…" following this with a zipping gesture across his mouth.

I paused to allow the full dream to break the surface of my mind. It bobbed up and sunk down, bobbed up again and sunk again, before it popped through, like a lovely, great trout leaping up from deep water to fly through the air. "Oh, there it is!"

I exclaimed and went on to describe what I was seeing.

"There was the brightest, bluest, most beautiful lake, tucked into the mountains, with the sweetest, tiny, tiny cabins along one of its shores, each little dwelling as inviting as the next, and a lovely, central gathering place for…"

"For singing…" murmured my friend, and then, remembering his pledge not to interrupt, added, "Oh, dear…"

"Oh, and the animals!" I continued enthusiastically, as more images surfaced from the night before. "So many animals."

"And the vista!" piped in my friend, clearly unable to contain his enthusiasm.

"…deep in the mountains," I whispered, mesmerized.

"Those mountains…" he added, rapturously.

"Oh, and that lake…like a great sapphire…" I continued, the images spilling into my clearing mind.

"Embraced by the oldest of old-growth forests," my friend fairly sang out.

"The trees! Like great giants!" I joined in ecstasy.

"Ancient ancestors!" he chimed in, clearly unable to contain himself.

"And the people…" I gasped, recalling faces, all such good faces. "The people…"

"Familiar?" he questioned.

"As if I'd known them forever." Several faces emerged, all so dear to me. "As if I had known them since birth."

"Or before?" my friend suggested.

"As if I had known them since time began."

"Or perhaps before there was such a thing as time?" he added.

I turned to my new friend, determined, as only a Willingly could be about the idea of an impending journey. "How will I find this place?"

"Well, now we've come to it, haven't we?" He shifted in his seat and grew rather practical, which seemed a bit of a stretch for him, as if he had forced himself into clothes that were far too stiff and formal. He cleared his throat, narrowed his eyes, and attempted to focus, trying to think how to give me my instructions without spoiling any of the secrecy which he was so poorly maintaining.

"Tomorrow morning," he began, "just after breakfast, you will step out of the hotel, and there will be…" He looked over at me, smiled warmly, wiped the smile from his face, and seemed to search for a word.

"Yes?" I encouraged.

"There will be…one…who will be waiting for you."

"One? Which one? One what?" I asked.

"You will be in excellent hands." He stopped and appeared to rethink his message. "You will feel quite comfortable with your guide. He will… shepherd you to the train station at the edge of the village, where you will find another who will offer guidance, and yet another on the train who will assure you of your direction and accompany you to your destination."

I waited for more information, but none arrived.

"Well, that might win the prize for the least informative directions I've ever been given."

"My tongue is tied by secrecy." He smiled broadly, and then thought for a moment. "There will be other travelers on the train, but they will not be going where you are going. The train is a rather slow-paced local affair, and all passengers will board and depart until the penultimate station, where the last of these travelers will disembark."

"Penultimate. Does that mean the second to the last?" I asked.

"Precisely. But you will remain on the train until it reaches its final stop, in the high alpine region, at which point you will depart the train and be met by…yet…one more."

"Oh, good gravy. I presume this figure will be as mystifying as the original one who is to accompany me to the station."

The man's eyes crinkled into a grin. "And you will trust her as profoundly as you have trusted all your companions along the way. She will carry you to the lake."

"The lake?"

"The lake."

We both took a moment to reflect on this still bright image, I from the recollection of my dream and my friend from what I presume were his memories of being there. We sighed in perfect unison before he continued. "You are not to bring anything. All will be provided."

"Nothing? Not even a toothbrush? I asked. "We Willinglys always bring our toothbrushes."

"If it would make you feel better, then by all means you must bring what you wish, but it is unnecessary. There is no need for any sort of preparation, and I hope you won't have the slightest apprehension over your journey. I assure you it will be quite pleasant—a trip into the mountains with everything provided for your comfort by the Choir."

"The Choir?"

My companion looked a bit shocked that he had let the word go from his lips. "Did I use that word?" he asked.

"I think you did, yes, the Choir." I repeated, "The Choir…" The word was deeply pleasing and brought up such sweet feelings from my lovely dream that I was moved to close my eyes and try and capture all that this word might reveal. "The Choir…" There was the warmest sensation in my chest, which grew and grew, slowly spilling out and over into my veins, warming my whole body, my head and feet, my hands. *The Choir, the Choir,* I thought to myself. The word was like sleep to exhaustion, food to hunger, a fireside to the ache of cold.

The Choir.

"I will go. I must go!" I said to my friend with perfect resolve, buoyed by the warmth rushing through my veins. "I am a Willingly and a Willingly never says no to adventure." I went on, flush with purpose, "I am a Willingly and a Willingly doesn't back down when faced with the challenge to hop on a train," I said, feeling very fine about myself and my heritage. And then I went a step further. "Now, I will tell you," I confided in my new friend, "there are those in my class at home—I attend a progressive school in Manhattan—who would never have the courage to accept such an offer. I can think of one girl in particular, but I…" I looked over at my companion and noticed a slight change. Was it a wince? And yet, I soldiered on…

"Her name is Margaret, and though she has had fun on many trips away from home, she tells me she dreads travel like the plague. Now I, being a Willingly, can't imagine such a…" I looked over at my friend again, and something was there, just a tiny movement, almost imperceptible, but I could swear he recoiled from me ever so slightly. "Are you all right?

My companion smiled politely. "Oh, yes, yes, dear," he assured me. "Continue."

"Well, I was just explaining the difference between me, being a member of the Willingly family, and my classmate, and how I…"

It was at this moment that suddenly, quite dramatically, the warmth and courage that had been coursing through my body turned off (as with a faucet, it simply turned off), leaving me stupefied.

What? I wondered. *What went wrong?*

My companion smiled politely at my confusion, as if he had been present inside of my head and had experienced the same reversal of emotion.

"You mustn't mind the play of feelings around your journey," the kindly man said. "It's perfectly natural to be a bit anxious. I assure you—you will be well cared for. Remember the Choir."

"The Choir," I said, hoping to feel the return of the warmth, the surety that had so emboldened me before. I closed my eyes, eager to retrieve some of the magic of that word, and remained like this, eyes shut, attempting to focus on the images from my dream. "The Choir, that lake, those animals…" I pronounced the words like incantations. "The Choir, the lake, those animals…" I continued to chant, hoping for a return of courage.

Unaware that the lights were flashing to signal the beginning of a new program, unaware that my companion had risen to leave, I struggled to recreate the feelings from my dream, but they would not return. I was in a fog of uncertainty. Eventually, opening my eyes, I could see the conference attendees filing in to return to their seats, and could see that the seat where my gentle friend had been seated was empty. I leaped to my feet to look where my good messenger had gone, but he was nowhere to be seen. Sitting back down, questions and concerns about what the next day would bring flooded into my mind, drowning my initial bravery. Whatever pluck had visited me had been plucked away. Oh, dear.

I sat heavily through the next hour's presentation without taking in any of the speaker's words. I can only remember that there was a rather vague discussion about how to start a conversation with a reptile. Whatever guidance was being offered, it had no power to penetrate my…my…okay, I must admit it…my travel anxiety.

Bravery is a gift, I have come to learn, and I try never to take it for granted. Even a Willingly can feel hesitant around travel. I learned that on this day.

But who were these Bright Ones the man had spoken of? Were these the same as the Choir? My mother had spoken to me of angels when I was younger. But like Santa Clause, I had come to view them as made up to entertain me as a child. Furthermore, why did the lovely feeling go away when I brought up my school friend and her fears? Did courage melt when it was compared to the courage of another?

So many thoughts raced through my head.

I don't remember that evening, but I do remember doing some tossing and sheet-twisting that night, finally dropping off into a deep sleep in the wee hours. Was I visited that night? Was it the Bright Ones that comforted me? I do remember a figure from my dreams that night, someone very noble and brave who was to be my guide to the lake, giving me such confidence in the next day's travels that when I woke, I found myself with a new sense of willingness. My fears appeared to be washed away. I was again willing to face the unknown. "Bring on the adventure," I said to my surroundings. "I am yours," I announced to the Bright Ones (whoever they were), "all yours."

2

M Y CHARMING mother sat across the break-fast table that morning eating muesli, as she pulled apart the previous day's predictions from the feline oracle from Duluth. "It seems that love will come quite suddenly, arriving something like any minute, and I am to be prepared to be swept off my feet. So reports the absent kitty-cat psychic from Minnesota. Tall, dark and handsome, the kitty promises, a perfect fit." And, pausing to eat her cereal, Louise reflected, "But, I must be will-ing, willing to…I can't quite recall…"

"Travel?" I suggested.

"Perhaps that was it. As if anyone need say that to a Willingly."

"This handsome man doesn't happen to come

with a daughter, does he?" I asked. "I would love to have a sister around the house."

"Maybe it isn't too late to put in a request for a sister for Whippoorwill."

We laughed together at the notion before my mother looked at me and cocked her head, as if suddenly remembering a detail of our schedule for the day. "I understand you are off to..." she searched for the word for a moment, and still unsure, offered, "summer camp?"

I smiled bravely and answered with a cheerful, "Yes, such fun!"

I must interject here that the words "summer camp" had never been vocalized between my mother and me in our years together, and I believe we both assumed never would be. We paused to take in the strangeness of the concept.

Louise was the first to speak. "Oh, and that lovely man, the one with the gentle face, has arranged everything. You needn't pack, apparently. 'But what about shoes?' I asked, and he assured me that all would be provided, and you will be back in time for us to travel home together, which is some time in the coming week. You needn't fret about me, I will be fine, as happy as a puppy in a shoe store. I hope they will supply you with the proper alpine boots, Whippoorwill." And then, remembering something the cat psychic had implied, added, "Oh, I remember what the feline from Duluth had said. She mentioned Africa…was it Africa? Maybe it was Arizona. No, no, I think it was a B word. Hm.… Oh, dear, maybe it was Baltimore. Maybe that will be our next adventure, Whippoorwill, Baltimore, Maryland. Now I'm feeling a pinch of disappointment. But I could have sworn that she mentioned an antelope, and there are no antelopes in Maryland. Whatever she was going on about, she made it clear that I was to stay very much open to the appearance of…of… Oh, dear, what was it…?" She trailed off and scratched her flamboyant head of hair.

It was at this point that three attendees of the Animal Communication Conference moved toward us to share our table. They appeared to be in the middle of a heated discussion about the apparent lack of communication they had managed to achieve between themselves and their housecats, and their hopes of changing that situation.

"If I've told him once, I've told him a hundred times," one of them said, pulling a chair out to sit at our table, "you really mustn't pounce on me when I come around a blind corner, as if I were a large mouse."

"I know exactly what you are talking about," her friend joined in. "I once sat my Charlie down and said to him, 'I'm simply not interested in being ambushed.' I expect to be able to walk freely throughout my house in relative peace."

I thought this was as good a time as any to begin my journey. Standing and walking over to my mother's chair, I kissed her pile of hair, told her I loved her, and steeled myself to move toward the exit of the dining room. Adventure awaited, and I was determined to face it like a Willingly.

Pushing my way through the front door of the hotel, I marched out bravely in three large strides, stopped, and planted my feet on the sidewalk. Ratcheting the appearance of daring up another notch, I rested my fists on my hips, and I looked about me. My seemingly confident gaze traveled to the left along the walkway, and to the right, as I drew in a powerful inhale and let loose an equally courageous exhale.

No one was there, not a single soul. *Well,* I thought, *this is either a stunning practical joke, or I ate my breakfast too quickly.* And so I took a seat on the bench to the side of the hotel door and waited. My view was of the east, with the sun just beginning to crest the lush, green hills, its rosy light slowly peeking over to grace the small Swiss town. And there I sat, taking in the warmth of the sun. I waited and tried not to panic. After a few minutes I decided to hum. "Hum di dum, dum," I murmured, in an attempt to seem self-possessed.

I don't know if it has ever happened to you, dear reader, that while thinking yourself alone, you slowly become aware of being watched. It's as if the focused attention of another set of eyes has a sort of substance to it, which can be felt, like something pressing in on you. This attentiveness felt a bit like warmth, like a blanket to a chill. I say warmth because the sensation was pleasing, friendly. But where was it coming from, I wondered? And then I saw him, directly across the street, sitting on his haunches, front legs straight, head raised, ears forward and alert. I couldn't identify the breed precisely, as I guessed there was a plentiful mixture of lineage. There was Burmese mountain, surely, considering the girth, and a bit of Labrador in the smile, and perhaps even a little dachshund thrown in for intelligence. But what was clear, what was absolutely apparent, was that the dog had inherited the friendliest qualities of all these breeds, and the result was an exotic combination of the comical, the noble, and highly pleasing. His jaw was slightly ajar, allowing for the sides of his great mouth to rise into a wide grin. He breathed gently and sniffed the air with the tip of his great leathery nose.

"Good morning," I said to him. "Are you the one I have been directed to meet today?" In answer to which he raised his back end to stand on all fours, looked both ways, up and down the road, and strode across the pavement to stand before me, allowing me a closer assessment. Such lovely, thoughtful eyes, topaz in color. There are some dogs that are just that—dogs, simply dogs—and there are others that are much more than dogs, or rather more of what the best of a dog could ever be. I was to learn more about why this was so, but for now, I could only guess at his role in my adventure. "You must be my guide," I suggested. "I believe you visited me in my dreams last night, and for that I am very grateful to you."

At this the great beast—and he was great in

every way, weighing perhaps one hundred and twenty pounds—stretched himself into a sort of low bow, legs straight before him, chin almost reaching the sidewalk, eyes lowered. He held this position for a moment before he raised himself with a dignified grace, looked me directly in the eyes, turned and began to move down the sidewalk toward the train station.

I hesitated for a moment, for a fear suddenly rose in me—oh, those little fears, so troublesome! A thought appeared, that perhaps this was an insanely orchestrated prank that would lead me into some sort of horrible trap. Sensing my doubt, the great dog stopped and turned to me. Acknowledging my apprehension, he sat and waited. I took a deep breath, recalled the courage of my ancestors, the encouragement of my dreams, and began to walk toward him. Convinced now of my following him, the dog moved on to walk through the tiny village. After a little while he began to pick up speed until we were traveling at quite a clip, with the two of us skipping our way toward the edge of town and the station.

My canine friend's pace, without check, grew more and more difficult for me to match. His legs were long and of course he had double the amount of them. I followed him at something closer to a trot now, mouth open and panting.

We passed a few people along the way, but I don't imagine anyone thought anything of our being together, and truthfully, it might have been difficult to see us as being connected to one another, as my guide was so far out in front of me.

At some point, feeling almost entirely out of breath, I called for him to slow his pace. "Could you, dear dog," I asked, "give me a moment to catch up?" The dog stopped, sat, and waited for me join him. I did so, stopping to lean over and pant for a bit. Holding my knees and catching my breath, I said to him, "I know I shouldn't complain. My ancestors, the Willinglys, will be rolling around in their graves in shame, but I am, though I know I don't act it, only eleven."

I paused for another moment, continuing to try and regulate my breathing. "And furthermore, my mother, if not always accompanying me, has typically arranged my life up to this point, and therefore the situation is new to me." I took in a great breath, staring into the curious face of my companion, whose head was tipping slightly from side to side as he looked searchingly into my tightly worried eyes.

It was then that the dog did something to completely win me over. Gently, very gently, he stepped toward me, and leaned his great body into my trembling one, his wide head pressing into my chest. And, as with any soft-coated, sweet-smelling beast that I have had the pleasure to befriend, I threw my arms around him and buried my face into his brow, breathing in his calming scent. We stood like this for just the right amount of time before I raised my head. He too straightened himself. I thanked him for his understanding and told him that I was ready now to proceed. Steadied at this point, with my hand on his shoulders, fingers twisted in his hackles, I moved along by my new friend's side toward the station at a much more reasonable pace.

Passing a few more souls on our way, we raised no concern, just a girl out walking her dog. But of course, I knew this to be exactly the reverse. We were a dog walking his girl, and this was to be something much more than a walk, something much, much more, and I must live up to my family inheritance and embrace whatever came next. One can't always depend on the courage of one's ancestors to come to one's aid when feeling wobbly, but I marched on, not precisely fearless but with a resolve to see the plan unfold.

As we approached the train station, I could see two sets of train tracks, one leading down from the great mountains and one leading up and into them. The train station itself was minimal, comprising a single room which provided one ticket booth and protection from inclement weather, the latter being something that was not at all necessary as the day was already proving itself to be a beauty.

Moving toward the ticket booth, I could just begin to gather my impression of the man inside. I could see that, like my messenger from the day before, this man's face was both extremely gentle and comfortably familiar. I would almost guess that I had known him as a child. I do see the irony of my describing him this way, as I was only eleven, but it was as if he might have smiled on me when I was an infant. His initial reaction, as my canine friend and I approached the booth, was clearly one of pure delight. A great, glad grin spread to the corners of his mouth. His expression, however, by the time we reached the counter, was tempered by what looked to be a purposeful attempt at seeming official. He chewed on the inside of his cheek, took the glasses off his face, and carefully polished them. After which he looked up, or down, as my head was slightly beneath the bottom sill of the booth, smiled again and quickly moved his attention to the dog.

"Sebastian. *Buongiorno, signore.*"

I turned to my companion. "Sebastian. So that is your name."

Sebastian yawned, as dogs will when shy of attention.

"A very dignified name," I complimented him.

Sebastian yawned again.

"*Allora, due biglietti per il Lago di Madre,*" the ticket man said, collecting two tickets from a drawer.

"Mother Lake? Is that where we are going?" I looked over at Sebastian for corroboration.

You might be surprised, dear reader, to discover that I knew a little of the Italian language, being only eleven, but my mother, as I have mentioned, is a romantic, and I was, at that time, attending a progressive school in New York City.

"*Ho detto quello?*" The kind man shook his head, coughed, and looked slightly rattled. "*No, no, Monte di…di…di…Grande.*"

"Big mountain?" I asked a bit suspiciously. "Could there really be such a pedestrian sounding place in this beautiful country?"

"*Allora.*" The man quickly changed the subject. "*Uno biglietto per la Signorina Weep-poor-wheel-luh Wheel-ing-lee.*" The man carefully read my name from the printed ticket, in the most charming accent. *"E uno per Sebastian."*

"Do dogs require tickets in your country?" I asked, and then, taking in what had been said, "But how do you know that I am Whippoorwill Willingly?"

His hand thrust itself out the window, handing me two tickets, saying, "Ees okay, *signorina*, ees okay," gesturing kindly with his entire body, smiling and winking, allowing me a moment to study him. The cut of the man's outfit was particularly peculiar. His shirt and jacket sleeves barely reached his elbows, his buttons were quite strained, his collar far too tight. It was as if, in his haste to dress that morning for work, he had accidentally grabbed his ten-year-old son's clothes for the day. Seeing my eyes widen with focus on his person, he began to wave us on our way. *"Buon viaggio, signorina!"* And then to Sebastian, *"Binario due, Sebastain, in dieci minuti. E in orario."*

At this, Sebastian turned to trot toward the door, and I scurried behind, catching up to open and hold the door for him.

The train was on time, as the ticket man had predicted. It crept into town, came to a complete stop, and the doors rolled slowly open. The door's opening had a sudden, electrifying effect on Sebastian. He sprang up and onto the train and turned to dash through the corridor. I leaped up the train steps and scampered after him. Sebastian moved along, sniffing the floor, sniffing, sniffing, passing up the occupied compartments, and sniffing farther and farther down the aisle of the car. When he reached the end of the first car, having apparently found no compartments to his liking, he leapt up to push the large button that would open the door at the end of the car, hopped across the divide between the cars, and leapt again to punch the next-door button, only to shoot into the second car, moving swiftly all the time, sniffing, sniffing. I followed frantically, occasionally smiling apologetically to the occupants of the rejected compartments, until at last, in the third car, he stopped, turned to look through the glass door of an empty compartment, found it to his liking, reached his great paw up to push the button, and shot through the door. Once inside, he bounded onto one of the bench seats and stretched his great body along the length of it. He then proceeded to roll about madly, as if suddenly discovering an infestation of nagging itches. He rolled and moaned and rolled some more. It really was a very undignified performance. Of course, I saw what he was up to. No one would dare to share our compartment with a mad, flea-infested canine. I will add that he chose the seat that traveled backward, allowing me to have the view of the oncoming scenery, which I thought awfully gallant of him. Sebastian settled, and in a moment, we were moving.

A local train ride through the grand foothills and up into the higher mountains of the Alps is such an upstaging experience to anything that might be of concern to the traveler that I would guess anyone's doubts about where they were going would be tossed away to wither on the tracks behind them. Assured that no one would come and join us, Sebastian leapt from his seat across from me to sit beside me and remained seated on his haunches for quite some time, as absorbed as I was with the view from our window.

I ohhhed and ahhhed at each picture-perfect scene: fields so green and so perfectly cared for. It was clear that the landscape had been groomed for the past several centuries by the perfect number of cows in each field. Pleasingly round and sturdy cows, I might add, mountain-climbing cows with velvet coats, tidy, even horns. We traveled slowly around and about and over and occasionally through the hills, passing such pleasing houses, always of a sensible size, never too big, just right. Some, I noticed, had tiny ladders designed for homeowner's cats to enter through upper windows. Every scene was worthy of a fairy tale. And, though it was August, the landscape was as green as the greenest April of home.

"Oh, I could live there, Sebastian," I would say of a little house on the side of an emerald-green hill. And, turning to the dog beside me, I would ask, "Couldn't you?" Sebastian kept his counsel, following my gaze. Another such gem would pop up in our field of vision and I would sigh, "Oh, look at that little farm! I would have the most perfectly cozy life by the side of that little stream, with those handsome cows, a couple of cats, perhaps a dog," turning to smile at Sebastian.

This was a favorite family pastime when traveling. The Willinglys can imagine living almost anywhere. Sebastian, when moved to agree with my choice of homes, would place his great paw on my knee. After a while it became, "Oh we could live there, couldn't we, Sebastian? On the side of that mountain, with that view. You and me and a couple of cows."

I have, since this day, found it interesting how quickly one can fall in love with a dog. I would give it under half an hour—if it's meant to be, that is. Now cats are a different story, and humans, well, humans rightfully require some time, often whole days, and some years. Humans are so often hidden inside themselves, aren't they, dear reader, making it difficult to know who it is you're meant to love, but dogs…dogs have nothing to hide. Sebastian was fast becoming like a member of the family, or…or what was the word the man used yesterday, the…the Choir, yes, the Choir.

I should mention the ticket collector before I go on much longer. Some of the oddest moments on this journey were the sudden and frequent appearances of the ticket collector. If this were a fable, she might have been one of the wee folk. She was tiny, somewhere in her sixties, rounded, like a small apple, and with the enthusiastic smile of a six-year-old.

When she first came to punch our tickets, the look of glee on her very round face seemed to light our little compartment with joy. It was as if, for one day, just one special day, she had been chosen, just she, out of hundreds of applicants, to play the role of a ticket collector on a train—something she had wished to be able to do her whole life—and this was the day.

She entered our little compartment, clasped her hands together, let out just a hint of a stifled squeal, and hopped several times in place. After which she composed herself slightly, remembering her lines, and said, "I *biglietti, per favore.*"

I searched in my pockets for the tickets as she smiled and chuckled to herself.

Finding the tickets and handing them to her, I watched her wrestle with the ticket-punching machine. This allowed me to study her. The uniform that she wore didn't appear to fit her at all. The pants spilled down over her shoes, the jacket reached her knees, and her hat swallowed most of her head. Her proficiency with the ticket-punching device was nonexistent. Finally giving up, she laughed and handed the tickets back to me, winked, and moved out into the corridor, winked again, and moved out of sight. I had to wonder whether any of the other passengers had found this character as odd as I had. Sebastian yawned, offering no opinion, and settled down for a nap. I couldn't have imagined sleeping through this journey and told him so. He groaned, stretched, and was asleep in seconds, lightly snoring at my side.

The train made frequent stops at first, but as we climbed farther into the mountains the tunnels grew longer, and the stops became fewer. Our elfish ticket collector walked past our compartment after each stop and gave us a wink and a nod, tipping her hat in our direction, but did not enter again until midday. At which point she arrived with an enormous grin, holding something with both hands behind her back. *"Hai fame?"* she asked.

This confused me for a moment, for I hadn't thought whether I was hungry or not. As I said earlier, nothing could override the appeal of the landscape out the window. While I thought of how to answer her, she swung a basket around from behind her back and plunked it down on the bench beside Sebastian. With eyes half open, the dog's nose began working, sniffing, sniffing, when suddenly his eyes popped open, and he rose from his slumber, hopped to the floor on all fours, and stood, staring holes through the basket with great intensity.

"*Qualcosa di mangiare,*" she announced, then clapped her hands, hopped once, and popped out the door.

The basket, once explored, held the most delicious little delicacies: small rounds of cheese, crusty bread, apples, and a bit of honey. But there was more. Squirrelled into a small paper bag were some sort of unrecognizable baked goods, the sight of which caused Sebastian to pant and whine with excitement, his front feet working back and forth. I hastily opened the bag and offered one of these nuggets to the great dog, and before I could blink, he had popped the thing into his mouth, swallowed it (without a single chew), and was staring at the bag, eagerly waiting for the next. This led to another, and then another, and yet another, and fifteen more others, until the bag was empty.

"All done, I'm afraid," I said to him, and crinkled up the bag. Sebastian stretched, hopped back up on the seat, and watched me explore my human food. The human/pet food line of delineation has always been a gray area in my thinking. He never begged—Sebastian was far too dignified for this—but he would not turn down a morsel. We finished the contents of the basket in what seemed to be under three minutes.

It was well into mid-afternoon when we arrived at what appeared to be the second to last stop. The last few passengers departed the train without anyone boarding to take their places, making Sebastian and me the only passengers left to travel. The train slowly moved forward, rising higher and higher into the great mountains. Our odd little ticket elf tripped up to our door, opened it, and stood with a look of unbridled anticipation. Her hands were clasped together, and her feet began to dance with joy.

"Grazie per il cibo, signora," I said, wishing to acknowledge the delicious food she had given us. *"E vicino? L'ultima fermata?"* I asked, wondering if we were near our destination.

"Si, si! Quindici minuti!" And then she dashed off toward the engine, laughing and clapping.

Fifteen minutes, she had warned. Oh my, I

thought. Had there been any instructions for what would happen when we arrived? I couldn't quite remember. Would there be anyone to meet us? "Another," the man had said. I would be met by "another." My chest was filled with butterflies.

3

I T WAS a good thing that I had nothing to gather before leaving our little train compartment, for Sebastian's anticipation of our arrival was barely controllable. He whined and threw his paws up on the window, panting with excitement. When the train did arrive at the station, it was immediately clear that it was not a station at all, for there was no building, no platform, just a small set of steps that seemed to magically align with the door of our car. When the train came to a complete stop, and the doors rolled open, Sebastian hurled himself out of our compartment, dashed to the door leading outside, and leapt over the steps and onto the ground. I followed frantically and landed next to him. After this display of impatience, Sebastian froze to take in the scene, moving only his nose and eyes to study the landscape before him, allowing me to do the same.

We had landed in grass. There was grass before us and all around us. The grass was cropped immediately around our feet, as if kept at a reasonable height by grazing animals but grew in height as the field in front of us spread out.

Having taken account of his surroundings, Sebastian did what so many of his kind will do when completely jazzed over their circumstances: He went for a puppy run. Racing around in joyful circles, tail tucked under, loping exuberantly, he made several broad laps around and around in a circle—some call this routine the zoomies—while I watched this spectacle of exuberance with a studied wonder. He seemed to have lost any degree of maturity that he might have assumed from being my guide for the day and became all unleashed youth. Like most animals after being constrained for a time, he was wild with freedom and mischief.

I have always been a rather disciplined person. My mother liked to warn me at the time that if I wasn't careful, I could be destined for a career as a school principal. At this point in my life, public displays of rambunctious behavior both puzzled and fascinated me. After all, I am an only child of a romantic mother. I have always taken my role of the anchor of the family seriously. At the time, I must admit, I could have benefitted from a good dose of abandon.

I stood watching Sebastian with curiosity for several minutes. I am not sure how many turns he made around and around his imaginary circle, but when he finally did stop running, I turned to discover that the train had quietly reversed from behind us and was on its way down into the valley from which we had risen. Only the steps remained behind.

"Oh," I exclaimed, dismayed. "And no one here to meet us."

Sebastian trotted over to me.

It was nice being an us, Sebastian and me, but I had hoped to be met by a someone, someone… perhaps human?

I took a deep breath and returned my gaze to the scene before me. The great meadow of tall grasses, waist high to the average adult, stretched out before us without a single path passing through. Behind this meadow were more meadows, delineated by lines of grand old trees, all leading up to the surrounding hills and backed by the great, ancient mountains. All was still, with just the barest hint of the sound of screeching metal from the receding train.

The only movement came from a group of cows that grazed in the far reaches of one of the distant fields. These were mountain cows, I presumed,

domestic animals which were released among the hills to spend the summer along with their calves before their owners came to fetch them in the fall to overwinter in warm barns. I could just barely hear them calling to one another, the mamas with their low murmuring "moos" and the young ones with their short high notes, "mah." On further study, one cow seemed to stand out as being rather taller than the rest, quite a bit taller, in fact. After a moment of scrutiny, I discovered this wasn't a cow at all, but a horse. A horse which was allowed the same freedom as the mountain cows. It grazed alongside the herd.

How unusual, I thought.

I watched this group of animals for a time, patting Sebastian's head, when Sebastian turned to look in the direction that was holding my attention. Suddenly his ears pointed forward, his breath stilled, his body froze, and one paw slightly rose from the ground. His ears then flattened as he began to move in the direction of the cows, very slowly, in what was certainly a stalking movement.

"Oh no, no, Sebastian, you mustn't chase those cows, they are domestic animals, they belong to someone." He paid me no mind but went creeping onward. "Oh no, no…" I groaned, and then tried calling him like a…well…like a dog. Clapping my hands, I sung out, "Come, Sebastian! Come here." I felt completely foolish, as if hailing a cab by raising one finger and whispering. It was hopeless. He was low in the grasses now, out of sight, but I could judge where he was by the slight movement of the surface of the grain. He moved in starts and stops, inching along and then darting forward when he thought the animals were not looking. He slinked and darted, slinked and darted. I watched in horror, unable to look away. I was more afraid for Sebastian than the cows, or the horse. What if he were kicked? The horse could certainly kill him with one swift blow to the head. He was clearly moving in for an ambush. The cows were placidly unaware, their calves, many of them, curled up and sunning themselves on the ground. The horse was grazing, head down, combing the ground.

Suddenly I felt very much alone; my new friend stalking danger, not a single human soul around me. What was my mother doing right now, I wondered?

A far too silent pause ensued before Sebastian shot out of the cover of the tall grass to speed across the back meadow. Suddenly there was total chaos, the cows sounding their alarms, calves in turmoil, the horse circling and then cutting away from the herd, bearing down on Sebastian. Sebastian not slowing his pace, coming for the horse, the horse rearing, landing, charging the dog. Sebastian looped around to nip the horse's heels. In one treacherous move he dashed right through the horse's legs. This was insanity!

I covered my eyes. "No, no, no, no," I groaned. But after a moment, I had to peek through my fingers. They were still at it, Sebastian barking, teasing, circling, with the horse squealing, bucking, chasing the dog, the dog chasing the horse, back and forth they went as they circled nearer and nearer to where I stood, Sebastian lost in the grasses but still audible, barking, barking, the horse tearing through the grass, barreling toward me. Sebastian finally broke through the grasses, coming for me, the horse pounding down after him, not slowing its pace, heading right for me. They were seven feet away from me when, sensing that they might crush me, both bodies, at full speed, lurched, stiffened, and came to a complete halt, front legs straight as trees, backends tucked under, turf flying, their front paws/hooves lifting off the earth for a moment before they dropped back down in unison. Standing before me, nostrils flared, they misted me with their steamy breath.

"Good garbanzos!" I shouted, shocked out of my reasoning mind. "You two are crazy dramatic!"

The horse, panting, blowing, body heaving, remained staring at me for perhaps three minutes before she slowly moved away to cool down. Taking her time, shaking, snorting, she eventually let out a soft whinny. I say she because her face was unmistakably feminine, gentle without being overly delicate. As with Sebastian, she seemed to be many horses stitched into one. She was not the picture of strength but was as fit as a fiddle. She was grayish, with a dark mane and tail, her ears a little too large, her tummy a bit too round for the length of her legs. She was not beautiful but possessed great beauty. I so wished I knew her name.

After a moment, the horse shifted and moved behind us to the tracks until she reached the set of steps I had used to descend from the train. She stood beside them. Sebastian nudged me on the hip to move forward.

"Oh gosh," I said. "Is this when we head for the lake?"

No answer from the horse.

"I feel a bit wrong riding when you two will be walking." Sebastian nudged me again, and I dutifully moved to the steps to climb up on my new friend, apologizing as I did so. "I'm not petite, you know. I'm going through my awkward years. It's a kind of lopsided growth spurt. My mother tells me that this is the only way I am to eventually find my individual beauty. She says it's a sort of requirement, this ungainly phase. But I do apologize."

At this point I found myself squarely sitting on the horse, something I had never before done, and I took careful note of the sensation. I will report several first impressions: I felt impossibly high off the ground, deliciously warmed by the horse beneath me, and enormously pleased. I was bareback, of course, and there were no reins to hold, so I tucked my hand in the horse's long mane. I hoped that she had gotten out of her system all the bucking and rearing for the day.

"I think I can do this if we keep it to a walk," I said, at which point we began to do just that and moved slowly through the field. The grasses were so high that they tickled my ankles, and before long I slipped my shoes off and shoved them into my pockets, allowing my feet to get to know the meadow. It was a delectable sensation. We traveled like this through the near meadow and into the next and the next, and into the one where the cows had been grazing. The field was empty now, apart from the birds skimming the tops of the grasses, with some of the birds occasionally flying very near to the three of us as we strode along.

At one point, a group of swallows, perhaps eight or ten of them, came circling nearer and nearer to our little group in what almost seemed to be choreographed movements. I presumed that our walk through the grasses was kicking up the insects, and the birds had come in to eat, but this performance seemed something more magical than food gathering. I could almost feel the bird's delight. "Oh, you pretty little darlings!" I sung out to them. "You are gorgeous!" The compliment seemed to cause their dance to become even more intricate, more beautiful. I watched, stunned into silence (which you may have gathered by now is unusual for me), as the birds danced around my head, rising, falling, twirling in place. They kept this up for some time before they flew off, leaving me breathless.

Eventually I took a long, slow lungful. "Okay, well, that was pretty wonderful. What else do you have up your sleeve?"

I'm not sure at this point with whom I believed I was communicating, but it felt as if whoever it was, this someone was part of everything that surrounded me, every animal, blade of grass, puff of wind. Perhaps, I reasoned, that after communicating with Sebastian all day, I might wish to expand my number of wordless friends to include all of my surroundings?

After half an hour or so, the meadowlands through which we walked began to descend gently, and we picked up a little path that traveled along the banks of a clear, swift stream. After a bit, the stream entered a forest of old growth pine. Our path was dense with a four-inch carpet of pine needles, allowing us to walk in perfect silence, as if on slippers, through the thick woods of blue-green trees. As we traveled, the stream hummed its watery, happy tune next to us, and at times, I thought, almost broke into song.

I don't know, dear reader, if you have noticed

that in nature there are certain things, growing, wave-lapping, blossoming things, that almost seem to demand that you stop and greet them. There are certain trees in Central Park in Manhattan, for instance, that insist on being properly recognized. My mother will say that to pass them without polite words would be as if you were to walk by someone's grandmother who had been particularly kind to you without saying hello. This little stream was such a being; it had a distinct personality. "Hello, dear stream," I spoke, looking down at its pebbly floor, its crystal water. "I think you must be the happiest, most playful creek in the world."

We walked on, in single file now, with Sebastian following.

At some point, a bit of worry came to visit me. I was plodding along, utterly pleased with my surroundings, when a thought arose. This will happen at the oddest of times. Sometimes I wonder whether there isn't a little alarm that goes off inside of me when I have been happy for too long. "Ding!" it seems to say. "Time to worry!" My little alarm went off when I tried to imagine what lay ahead for me. I wondered if I would feel comfortable where I was going, wondered if I would find friends, wondered if I were headed for discomfort and homesickness. I was beginning to spiral down into worry-land when I heard it. I could swear that the stream chuckled. And, as swiftly as it had arrived, my disquiet sailed away from me on the breeze like a paper airplane.

"Sebastian?" I asked, turning back to look at him. "Do the streams in this part of the world have voices?"

Sebastian kept his own counsel as he trotted through the bed of pine needles, his nose working to detect the scents of his surroundings. He seemed to belong to this place, in this forest, as if he had sprouted from the piney loam beneath us. We walked on, through this valley between the mountains for several hours. Occasionally, when rounding a bend in the path, I would have a glimpse of the surrounding high mountains, but for the most part the trees were so thick and dense, with branches reaching across our heads to greet one another, that my view was quite limited. There were several times when I had to duck to avoid being swept from my seat by low hanging branches.

The horse was careful of me, slowing her pace to move under particularly low branches so that I would be sure to avoid a head banging. Once we approached a particularly low-hanging branch that had a large gray owl resting on top of it. I assumed that the owl would take off in alarm as we approached. We came closer and closer, but the bird remained still, as it steadily grasped the branch beneath with its talons. Finally I ducked my head and lay myself on the neck of the horse to travel under the branch, and still the owl kept his place on the branch. Having made it under the overhang, I turned around to look, and there sat the bird, completely at ease.

Sebastian stopped under the branch to look up at the bird, sat back on his haunches, and let out one sharp bark. The owl rose up from its branch, flapping its wings briefly, and then landed back down on the branch. Sebastian picked himself up and continued on his way. Mystifying behavior for both species.

Where was I, I wondered?

After a while in these woods, I couldn't help but feel a fondness for certain trees that we passed as if they were old friends. I could swear that some of them had a sort of protective interest in me. I know this will sound odd, but they almost seemed related to me, like ancient ancestors from my mother's side of the family. As we rode by them, I could almost imagine them saying, "Oh, that's Louise's child," as if we were at a reunion of sorts. "Still a sapling, but coming along…"

Was I making all of this up out of loneliness? I didn't think so. Ever since I had climbed up on the horse, I had felt something more akin to sisterliness, a sort of easy comfort with my animal companions, and I presumed that this feeling was inspiring me to embrace all my surroundings. Is it possible to feel a kinship with trees? With a stream? I did so that day, on that ride through that forest.

At some point along our journey down this path, we passed a fox who had come down to the opposite side of the stream to drink. He stopped drinking, sat back on his haunches, and watched us pass, his gaze moving from one side to the other at the slow pace of our movement along the path.

"Hello, brother fox," I said, for I was getting more used to this familial feeling. Now it might have been my imagination, but I would swear the fox bowed his head to me. I twirled around to look at Sebastian's reaction. It is one thing for a dog to pass up chasing a bird, but a fox is an irresistible temptation for any dog. Sebastian walked by without drama. And, again, it might have been my very active mind playing tricks, but I could have sworn that he answered the fox's bow with his own, nodding his head in greeting.

What was this place, I questioned?

After a long while, the path began to move away from the stream and rise up and out of the woods. We finally broke out of the shaded canopy of evergreens and into more meadowlands, doing so as the sun was perhaps an hour from setting. The path led up to the foot of a great hill, which was gently sloped at the bottom but grew steeper and steeper as it rose to its top. The horse turned up the slope and seemed to head directly for the summit.

She walked with a lighter gait now, effortless. At one point on our ascent we moved toward a herd of deer, perhaps a dozen in total, with does and late-summer fawns. The deer remained grazing as we approached and, as with all the wildlife that we had encountered on this journey, they did not move away as we came nearer, eventually allowing us to walk through them, almost as if we were invisible.

We were so close that one of my feet grazed the ear of a yearling. Without causing the slightest of reactions, the young deer twitched its head as if an insect had landed.

Now it is one thing to be camouflaged on the back of a horse (a prey animal), riding through a group of prey animals, but to be accompanied by a dog (a predator animal) and elicit not the slightest alarm, no foot stomping or snorted warning, was remarkable. And was it my mind again, playing tricks, or did the horse nod to one of the does? And did the doe nod back in recognition?

As I had mentioned, the higher we rose on the mountain, the steeper grew the grade of the slope, and the lighter grew my ride. I could feel her growing playful, as if itching for a run. And, as I had no reins or saddle, I had wondered what might happen if my horse decided to take off with me. The moment after I had this thought, as if on cue, the horse lifted and almost seemed to fly up the hill like a bird. I use a bird as an image because it was such a smooth, airy sensation, as if her hooves never touched the earth, and it was over before I had time to be terrorized.

Suddenly, there we stood on top of the hill,

looking back over the valley through which we had been traveling. I could see the forest of trees, and I believed I could almost see the distant meadows where we had begun our trek. It was all so beautiful in the diminishing light of the late afternoon sun. And then the horse turned, and I with her, and oh my, such a stunning scene lay beneath us. A jewel of a small lake sat nestled in a bowl of bright green hills, covered with dense forest, all of which sat inside another, larger bowl of majestic mountains. A small cerulean blue jewel inside a majestic setting. I use the word majestic, but there was nothing kingly about these mountains, nothing grandiose. The scene was all gentle beauty, all friendliness, like the arms of a great, tender parent, and it felt as if this gentle one was loving the three of us through this place of beauty. I took several deep breaths, unable, for the moment, to speak. A rarity for me. Until I was able to whisper one word.

"Home."

4

OH, THE lake, the lake, the lake…gleaming sapphire, astonishingly, thrillingly alive. If there was any question of whether or not I should vocalize a greeting to a being in nature, this lake put that to rest. I could not have kept myself from speaking.

"Oh my," I blurted, awestruck, "Good afternoon, you beautiful one."

What came next was entirely unexpected. To my great and joyful surprise, the lake glistened in response. When I say it glistened, I mean the lake clearly responded to my salutation with a slow-rising display of sunlight, playing across its surface, as if growing in intensity from a thousand tiny spots of light to that of a thousand bright candles, flickering, orange, red, yellow, blue, playing with every hue of the rainbow before slowly receding and diminishing back into its original natural beauty.

Oh," I gasped. "Oh, that was something," I sputtered, "that was really something."

The three of us stood in the afterglow of this thrilling performance for a moment—I as stunned as I can ever remember being—when the horse beneath me let out a tremendous screaming whinny. The call shook me violently out of my spell and nearly unseated me. As I attempted to regain my balance, from the valley below I heard, as if in echo, the answering whinnying calls of other horses in distant but equal strength. In response, my horse let out another piercing call, glad and powerful, followed by the others responding in equal gladness. I guessed this group to be perhaps a dozen in number. The sound of their calls began to spread out, indicating that they were on the move. They continued to cry out as they rose up from the lake valley, swiftly rising toward the summit. At the same time, the horse beneath me began to dance, trembling, barely able to contain her joy.

"I think this is my time to disembark," I declared as I slipped my shoes back on, twisted myself around on my belly (legs to one side), and dropped to the ground. And, oh boy, if you've ever ridden a horse for many hours, having never ridden a horse in your life, you will understand the sensation. I've never felt so suddenly, impossibly short. At the same time my body felt as rigid as a broom handle. I was just wondering whether I would ever be able to walk again, given my stumpiness and my stiffness, when the sound of the stampeding hooves reached my ears, and I shot off like a rabbit

for the nearest tree. A great oak stood by itself on the top of the hill, and I lurched into its embrace, hugging it for dear life.

"Oh, good tree, save me!" I pressed my head against its trunk and closed my eyes, hoping to disappear into its mottled bark. But something—I believe it was the gladness echoing up from the valley—encouraged me to peek through my fingers to watch for the arrival of the charging horses.

The horses from the valley finally appeared on the plateau of the hill, galloping at a great pace. My horse joined them, rearing joyfully. Sebastian, who, up to this point, kept his cool, lost all poise: barking, hopping, circling. The herd bucked and darted, chased each other playfully. I clung to my tree, wide-eyed, quivering. Eventually the herd began to calm, slowing its pace to a canter. Easy now, graceful, necks loosely swinging, they formed into a line and began to circle the hill, with me and my new friend the oak tree in the middle. Sebastian joined the circle, which now numbered fourteen creatures: twelve horses, Sebastian and a…I couldn't quite make it out. It was small, nearly as small as Sebastian, but it wasn't a canine, it was more equine. And then it made its call, and there was no doubt. A great, resounding *hee-haw* pierced the air. It was a donkey, a very small donkey with tremendous ears. Its bray cut through all the other sounds the beasts were making, piercing through the pounding, whinnying, and barking. Once released, the bray repeated and repeated, "Hee-haw, hee-haw, hee-haw," the donkey howled, tossing its head, kicking up its hooves, looking like the happiest creature alive. The pace of the cantering beasts began slightly to diminish, as the animals tightened in toward me and my oak. I clung to the great tree, wishing its branches were lower that I might climb up and into its arms. The animals were slowing to a trot now, blowing through loose lips, with the donkey finally able to lessen its furious speed. Eventually they slowed to a walk, and then to a standstill, and all turned to face me directly, heaving their great chests, blowing, shaking their necks, coming to rest.

"Good gazpacho!" I heaved in unison with them. "You guys can sure put on a heart attack show!"

We stood for some time, catching our breath, taking each other in, before I spoke again.

"Oh, look at you all," I gasped. "Such a perfectly stunning collection of creaturehood!"

In truth, they were a quirky group of equine cake mixes. Again, not individually beautiful, but each possessing great beauty. I loved them all, instantly, equally, all of them, forever and ever.

It was at this point that the donkey, rather shyly, made a step or two toward me, and then another, and another, approaching in careful stages. And oh me oh my, what a darling little beast! She was all ears and head, balanced on four tiny hooves, wrapped in the shaggy rug of her nut-brown coat. Her eyes—for again, there was no doubt that she was a she—her eyes made me want to hug her in the worst way. Either hug her or weep, I couldn't decide which. It was as if a piece of my heart which had been missing had returned.

I thought of my mother and our visits to Central Park over the years to the children's petting zoo. There was a donkey there who we used to visit. This donkey, also a miniature, was the picture of kind patience: allowing her visitors endless sessions of ear rubbing, scratching, patting, perfectly patient with babies poking, children learning to be gentle, adults reliving their childhoods. She seemed to be made of the substance of peace. I had loved her for years when, one day, we went to visit, and she was no longer there. Three young donkeys had taken her place.

My mother would never treat a child as if she couldn't understand the concept of a spirit moving out of this world and into the next. "Our donkey has likely relocated from her earthly home to her eternal home, darling," she said to me. "She's translated into her finest donkey body and has taken her wealth of caring to the child spirits in the world of perfect love." And then she added encouragingly, "Let's be happy for her, shall we? In the meantime, look at these three characters." She gestured to the young donkeys. We named them Eeny, Miney, and Moe, and continued to visit the little rascals whenever we could.

The donkey on the hilltop had continued to move toward me all the while and was almost in front of me when I returned from my memories. At which point, she moved directly up to my belly and reached her great nose to nuzzle me, finally taking a piece of my sweater between her teeth and giving it a gentle tug.

"I'm ready to follow, if that is what you are asking," I said to her. After which she moved to my side, looked over at me, and began to move toward the edge of the hill. Sebastian trotted over to take his place at my other side. The horses parted so that we could walk through their circle, and the three of us took a moment to pause at the crest of the hill before beginning our descent. I looked back to see that the horses had relaxed, broken their circle, and were grazing together, gently pulling at the grass and snorting.

After which we turned to make our way into the valley.

As we moved down the steep slope, we came to areas of uneven ground, but I was well balanced with my two animal friends at my sides, my hands resting on their shoulders. In this way we traveled slowly down the decline toward the lake.

Oh, the lake! We took many breaks to view this marvel. The sun was quite low now, and the valley began to take on a golden quality, enchanting everything it touched. The greens of the pines were like emeralds, the sky a rose quartz, the lake was so filled with colors that I couldn't distinguish between them. They shimmered like silk.

We eventually moved down and into the thick, old-growth forest, where the sunlight pierced through the branches of the pines like rose-colored swords, with dramatic streaks of light. The soil was rich and well-cushioned with pine needles. With little undergrowth and no need of a path, we wove through the trees, side by side, traveling through a huge cathedral of giant trees. All sound of our footsteps was perfectly muffled. The woods felt holy, sacred, so much so that the three of us wouldn't have dared to walk through in any state but silence. A voice would have destroyed the power of its presence. I walked along, thinking of the rare times when such silence had been available to me in my life up to this point. I would have to do something about this in my adult life, I vowed. I must someday live either in or near the deep woods.

I cannot say how long we walked in this dense quiet, but eventually the grade of the hill leveled out and I guessed that we were nearly on the bottom of the bowl of the valley. Through the diminishing light, I began to see the outline of a handful of small, rounded structures in the distance, each with very pointy roofs and tucked into its own nest of trees. The closer we came to these dwellings, the better I could see them. There seemed to be no more than a dozen, all with their own privacy but near enough to their neighbor to be friendly. Each little building was similar in construction but with touches of individuality. They blended in so beautifully with the landscape that they appeared almost to have grown from the soil beneath them. Indeed I was to learn that the walls had been sculpted from the clay of the lake and smoothed into rounded structures with carved-out, deep-silled windows and doors. The roofs were made of wood, covered with a dense blanket of moss. Each small structure was of a different but similar color echoing the woods surrounding: rich browns, deep greens, and golds.

At some point during our approach we came to a path which led to a three-way fork. Without hesitation, my donkey friend chose the middle path. I followed, behind her now, as the path was narrow. We soon came to another fork, with the same number of choices of direction, and again my donkey chose the middle path. Again I followed, with Sebastian on my heels. It was this path that eventually led to the dearest little hut, a deep yellowy-gold, thick mossy, steeple-like roof, surrounded by a rich carpet of ferns. It was darling, enchanting, perfect.

In the half light, I could see that the door of the

hut stood open. In silhouette from the soft light spilling out from inside stepped the slight figure of an elegantly dressed woman. From our distance, I could make out a simple, comfortably draped tunic worn over a pair of loose pants. A rope belt encircled her waist. As we came nearer, I could see that the color of this simple outfit was a beautiful periwinkle blue, the color of a tanzanite, and the belt was secured by a striking little gem which appeared to be the color of the lake, a color that I had not yet begun to pin down. It was blue, yes, but as I have mentioned, it seemed to hold all color. The woman glided gracefully out of the door on soft, flat shoes, with a look of such pleasure I could barely meet her gaze.

"Whippoorwill!" She clasped her hands and beamed. "Dear Whippoorwill."

I thought perhaps it was a good time to apologize for my accumulating embarrassments. "Oh my," I sighed. "You are the fourth person who I have met in the past twenty-four hours who appears to know me, and I must confess, though you look familiar, I cannot place you. I think it's my age, you know. Some people might have met me before my memory arrived. Something that I would guess occurred when I was about four and a half years old. I hope I don't seem rude."

"Oh, dear," she smiled. "No, it was long before you were an infant that I knew you, but this may remain a bit of a mystery to you. I see that you have met Sebastian and Pearl."

"Pearl!" I turned to the donkey and stroked her between the ears. "What a lovely name! Thank you, Pearl, for bringing me here."

"This is to be your home for the week," the gentle lady said. "Sebastian and Pearl will stay with you. One inside and the other outside."

"Oh my," I answered with keen delight. "Such a darling, dear place!" And then remembering my manners, "And what is your name?"

"You may call me Sunshine, that is what my name means in Hindi."

"Sunshine," I said, and then thinking further, "Does that mean you are from India?"

"Yes, it mainly does. I suppose I shouldn't be impressed with your knowing this, but I am."

"I attend a progressive school in Manhattan. We're very global."

She smiled at this, with a subtle crinkling of her eyes, giving me a moment to study her. She had a striking face, long noble nose, shiny black hair worn in a loose braid, deep-brown eyes beneath great domed lids. Her expression held several qualities at once. One, I guessed, was a studied intelligence, and the other might have been the weight of some concern, though she did not seem gloomy by any means, only grounded by something, some sorrow perhaps. I found her immensely fascinating.

Sunshine continued speaking, "I have come here with my son, Mayan. It's our day to serve."

"Serve?" I asked.

"Yes, all visitors here are granted one day of service. It's the most satisfying day of them all." And added, "My son is grooming Cowslip after her long ride."

"Cowslip? Is that the name of the horse who brought me here?"

"Yes," Sunshine answered. "She carried Mayan here as well. She is particularly careful with children."

"Does your son know how to groom a horse?" I wondered.

"He's learning. He's only six," Sunshine explained. "He was the one who was invited here. I rode in on his coattails, so to speak."

"And where did the nice man find you?"

"Humphry?"

"Is that his name? Oh, I like that name."

"He wrote to us in India, through the mail."

"And you came all the way from India, prompted by a letter?"

"There were instructions."

"Yes, but…"

Sunshine continued, "Mayan had expected the invitation."

"Had he?"

"He is quite special, Mayan. He knows things," she added, smiling to herself. "You will meet him soon, in little over an hour, in fact. In the meantime, I have run a bath for you and hung your clothes in your room. Your shoes are just inside."

Sunshine turned to walk inside the door, and I followed with Sebastian on my heels. Once inside, my new friend pointed out the most inviting pair of low, flat boots resting just beside the door. They looked as if they might have grown from a tree, as if made from the softest of spring leaves. I immediately removed the shoes I had on, in deference to these masterpieces, and moved inside to explore my new quarters.

We were in a sitting room with a lively little fire in its stone fireplace. The room would fit perhaps three people comfortably, with low cushioned easy chairs surrounding the fire. To be precise, the room would fit three humans and a large dog, for there was a very cozy looking dog bed near the hearth. I moved to the fire to warm myself, as my feet sunk into a soft, thick rug. The room was so warm and inviting that I felt as if I were being hugged by its atmosphere. Breathing in the scents of the burning wood, the slight chill of the evening began to leave my body.

Eventually, turning to warm my back against the fire, I gasped. There was a large round window with a bench seat along its sill, which looked out over the lake. Oh, the lake, the lake in the alpine sunset…. It transcended every thought, every question, all curiosity. Have you ever felt so warmed in your heart, by a story you have heard, a book you read, or an act of great kindness, that you feel your chest might melt into a puddle of peace?

Sunshine watched my reaction. "Yes, the lake… You will never grow any less amazed by this lake. The bath you are about to take is filled with water from her."

I looked at Sunshine. "Her?"

"Yes." Her face softened, and she joined me in a moment of gazing and awe. After a moment she said, "Now I must leave you to bathe and dress. Your bedroom and bath are just in there." She gestured toward a door leading into another room. "I will return for you in an hour to take you to the gathering house. Are you all right on your own? Sebastian will stay with you, and Pearl will remain just outside."

"Oh my, yes, yes, this is all so perfectly delicious!"

"Have a quiet soak, and I will see you soon," Sunshine said, and slipped out the door, pulling it shut behind her. I moved to the great window to watch her walk away. Sunshine moved slowly, mindfully, looking up into the trees as she went. I had guessed that she wouldn't be the sort to dash through such beauty, and I was right. She moved as an owl will fly, gently, consciously, and I suspected her movements were equally as soundless. Just as this thought arose in my mind, an owl, a proper owl, large and gray, swooped down from the forest and swept the air above Sunshine's head. Was it the same owl from the woods earlier, I wondered?

Sunshine stopped and looked up. The owl circled back around and swooped a bit lower, almost touching the hair on her head. She raised her hands up above her. Was she afraid, I wondered? Then the owl came back for a third pass, this time coming so near to her upstretched fingers that his chest feathers appeared to graze them. After which the owl flew up the path, with Sunshine seeming to follow, as if he had asked her to meet him up ahead.

What was this place?

I stood in astonishment as the light receded. Finally, turning away from the window, I noticed Sebastian standing at my side, watching me.

"Oh, Sebastian," I said, taking in a long breath. "We could live here."

5

I WILL ALWAYS have a difficult time trying to describe this first bath in the lake's water. I've wondered since whether I might have fallen asleep during it, for I remember stepping into and out of the bath, but little more. I do know that I entered as a long-traveled, weary passenger and emerged completely restored, as if I had had a layer of resistance and concern permanently removed from my spirit. I felt all newly born, like a three-month-old puppy. I do, though the memory is vague, recall hints of what occurred during my time in that bath. At one point I would swear that my blood had turned to sparkling water and had gone fizzing through my veins. At another point I sensed my muscles release all at once, like the little toy wooden animals you find in Switzerland, held together by string, and when released by pushing the button beneath, collapse into a heap of tiny wooden body parts. I know I put my head under the water at some point, but at no point did I use any sort of soap. There was no need. The magic of the water was enough to shine the crustiest coin.

When I eventually heard a gentle knock on the front door, followed by Sunshine's voice, I was sparkly clean, with perfectly dry hair and comfortably clothed in a similar version of Sunshine's outfit. My tunic, which was draped over soft pants, was a pale yellow, and included a simple rope belt that wrapped around my middle. This held the most fascinating closure of an embedded crystal, the reflection of our lake, shining on my hip. A thin wool cape hung on the side of the door for the cool evening. I took this down from its hook and pulled opened the door.

After taking a moment for my eyes to adjust to the dark, I leapt back in terror. It wasn't Sunshine that caused this reaction, or the boy next to her, but the creature that stood with them. I have since learned that it is a type of leopard found in India, commonly known as a black leopard, a massive beast with bright yellow eyes, striking, overwhelmingly powerful looking. I stood gasping, unable to catch my breath.

Mayan was the first to speak. "Don't let her worry you, she is all gentleness." He touched the great cat on her cheek, and she turned to lick his hand. "Her name is Ruby. You may pat her if you wish, Whippoorwill."

Did everyone know my name in this place? I hesitated, then asked, "May I reserve this privilege for a later date?"

Mayan laughed the bright laugh of a six-year-old. "Of course," he said, staring straight before him, more through me, it seemed, than at me. In fact, his eyes had not moved since he arrived at my door. "We were a bit fearful when we first arrived, weren't we?" he continued, still with unmoving eyes, not turning to his mother for corroboration. "And when Ruby first came to nuzzle my hand, I couldn't make out what sort of creature she was. But I knew she was gentle, the way she moved in to lean on me, the way she smelled of grass and flowers. It was when she made a low growling noise that I knew her to be one of the great cats. I'm told that she is all black with yellow eyes, but when I see her, I see the deepest of reds, a rich, rich, ruby red."

Of course, I understood at this point that Mayan was blind. Perhaps not blind from birth as he must have known color at some point, but his eyes were sightless now. Though clearly his inner eyes were very sharp.

"We've come to fetch you for dinner, Whippoor-will," Sunshine interjected. "I imagine Sebastian and Pearl are eager for their dinner as well."

At hearing the mention of dinner, both Sebas-tian and Pearl let out their distinctive joyful sounds, with Sebastian barking and Pearl braying with great might. Ruby stood motionless, serene among the chorus of excitement.

Sebastian bounded out the door and ran ahead, Pearl followed kicking up her heals, and Ruby turned slowly to move down the path with Mayan walking at her side, his hand resting on her shoul-ders. I closed the door behind me and fell in with Sunshine, moving to the first fork in the path and taking the path on the right this time.

"And what did you think of your bath, Whippoorwill?"

"I wish I had words to tell you what I thought. Do you imagine I will ever find those words?" I asked.

"She is quite mysterious, our lake," Sunshine concurred. "I have thought that perhaps it is a good thing that we cannot see her in all her beauty at night. It gives us a break from her splendor."

"Yes, I understand what you mean. It's difficult to think of anything but her while the sun shines."

"Mayan sees her, though not through his eyes, and seems to understand her better than anyone."

"And what does he say about her?"

"She is our mother, he explains, she is mother to us all."

I couldn't speak for a moment but took a great sighing breath. We walked on in silence. We had walked for some time, all of us, soaking in the peace of the surrounding forest, when I felt the top of my head being very lightly ruffled as if a single puff of wind had tussled my hair. I looked up and saw the great owl which I had seen earlier over Sunshine as she had walked away from my little hut.

"Ah, Rembrandt," laughed Sunshine.

"Rembrandt?"

"Yes, he is my Pearl, my Ruby."

"Then Pearl is my…?"

"Companion animal, if you will, representing a quality of your nature, perhaps yet to reveal itself; your gift to the world."

"A donkey?"

"In some cultures the donkey represents peace and patience. I'm told that in the Bible there is a donkey through whom God speaks. In your own life, the donkey has represented tolerance. I refer to the donkey in the petting zoo."

"You know about that donkey?" I asked.

"Yes, of course. Pearl is…" she began but stopped herself. "Some knowledge is shared among us before the next friend arrives, especially having to do with the soul's gifts. We are all encouraged to open and share our gifts. I understand you enjoy singing, Whippoorwill."

"Oh, I love to sing. I sing in a choir at home."

"Then you will enjoy our evening," she suggested with a wink.

The owl circled and swooped down toward us again. "Hello, Rembrandt!" I called out. He twirled in the air as if in answer to my voice, and dove down again, lightly brushing my head

"He's an acrobat," Sunshine said, proudly.

"And what gift does Rembrandt represent for you?"

"He is a barn owl. Barn owls are devoted partners, devoted to their families. I would say that the quality he represents is devotion. But this can mean many things."

I looked ahead at Mayan with his hand on Ruby, and imagined being the eyes for a blind child and what devotion this would require.

"I know what you are thinking, but that particular act of devotion brings more joy to me than you can imagine, certainly more joy than effort. The male barn owl will feed his entire family, hunting between twenty-five and thirty mice a night. They are tireless in their devotion. They are so devoted to their mates that often, when one passes away, the other will turn away from the world, refuse to eat, and pass soon into the next world themselves."

"Does Rembrandt have a mate?"

"He did, once, but he has already had his journey here."

I looked at her in confusion.

"You will understand this soon," she assured me.

"I hope to understand many things from being here."

We walked on in silence for a while, stopping occasionally to listen to the sounds of the settling forest. This was to become one of my favorite pastimes in the forest around the mother lake: walking in silence, with a friend. There was no awkwardness to being silent in another's company in this place, as there often is elsewhere. It was as if everyone who visited had been given permission to allow the forest to speak first. This was a lesson that I was to learn many times a day in this place. It has stayed with me in the years since this time, and I suspect it will remain a valued skill for the rest of my life.

Mayan and Ruby were so comfortable with this atmosphere of quiet listening that they hardly ever made a sound while walking in the forest. And, in particular, Mayan did not feel the need to chatter to Ruby. They would stop along the path often and, as they were ahead of us, we would take a moment to stop as well and discern what might have arrested the attention of this unlikely pair. And, though these halts seemed as if they had purpose, we could not always detect the reasons for them. Once Mayan stopped and let out a great peal of laughter. And, turning to Ruby as if she had just told him a very fine joke, he leaned over to grab his knees in hysterics. Mayan's laugh was like a mad woodpecker's, completely unrestrained and infectious. Ruby would allow herself a rather undignified leap into the air, and settle back to his side, allowing for his hand to rest back on her shoulders. Sunshine and I had to stop and join in this infectious laughter before moving on.

We hadn't been walking too terribly long through the woods before we began to see the twinkling lights of a building in the distance. As we approached, I could see that this was a larger, though similar, structure as the little hut where I was to sleep. The two were alike in rustic comfort, but this building had slightly larger windows, each shining with a deep rose light. But it wasn't the light that so captured my attention on our approach but the sounds. It was music, choral music, in perfect harmony, perhaps made by three or four voices, and it was a song that was unfamiliar to me and at the same time known to some part of me. I understand that this makes little sense, but I was growing more and more used to things not making sense to any part of me but my heart, which seemed to know much more than my mind. I've since come to understand that it's often our hearts that first understand things, with the mind eventually catching up. But the oddest thing about this song was that it was punctuated by accents of tones that I could not recognize. These might have been produced, I thought, by foreign instruments which were unfamiliar to me.

As we neared, some of our group began to join in with the singing. This was performed softly at first. It began with Sebastian, who made a low, moaning hum, then Pearl punctuated Sebastian's moan with a single note from her bray: "Hawwww," she seemed almost to vibrate. Mayan then began to sing in his lovely child voice, and Ruby made low guttural purring sounds beside him. Eventually Sunshine sang out with the purest of alto voices. Familiar with her part, she wove her splendid voice with precise confidence, braiding her harmonies with the other voices in intricate complexities.

I had rarely heard such close, haunting harmonics. The memory of my bath surfaced, and I had a vague notion of having listened to this very music while bathing in the lake's water. We approached the building swiftly, as if carried on the enthusiasm of the music. By the time we entered the gathering hut, I found that I was singing along with the rest, adding my voice to the soprano line of the piece. After a moment I became aware that I was singing in a language that I did not know. And, as we moved into the next song, the language would change, and my understanding with it.

We continued like this for some time, moving around the world with our choice of songs, each of us entirely absorbed in joyful chorus. After a while I could relax into the music, which allowed me to study the faces of those around me.

An ensemble of diverse spirits stood in a circle serenading one another. When we joined the group, we were six humans and seven species of animals, with the addition of Sebastian. Rembrandt had flown in to sit on Sunshine's shoulder, making the strangest sounds of all: clicking and screeching and hooting. The addition of his voice made everyone smile. Pearl's braying was by far the loudest of the voices, yet oddly it seemed to blend beautifully.

I don't want to overburden you, dear reader, with remembering everyone's name and their companion animal, so perhaps it would be best to introduce my new friends one at a time. I found myself standing next to a girl, near to my age but a bit older, who stood with her hand on the back of an antelope of some sort. The girl's most notable attribute was a pair of legs the length of stilts, or so they seemed to me. She turned to smile at me, and reached out to stroke Pearl, who stood between us. Keeya, for that was her name, sat next to me that first evening, and I learned a little about her and her delicate female lechwe, a water-loving antelope found in the country of Botswana, where Keeya lived. Keeya had a gentle contralto voice that seemed to anchor the rest of us to the earth, as if she sang for the earth, sang for all the growing things that sprouted from the earth. In truth, these songs were so soothingly simple that it was as if they had sprung from the earth's untouched forests and fed by a thousand pristine lakes.

As she sang, Keeya made small subtle movements with her feet, as if the song was also meant to be an understated dance, barely noticeable. My own feet picked up the rhythm and began to move as Keeya's did, with the rest of the company eventually adopting the movement as well. We sang and moved like this for thirty minutes or so, I would guess, changing songs frequently, before we came to the end of the repertoire and stood smiling, listening now to the silence.

It was Sunshine who broke the spell. "And now it's time for the animal kingdom to have their dinner." If Sebastian and Pearl had made a racket earlier when the idea of dinner had been raised, the seven animals present were a riot of noise, leaping and circling and finally dashing after Sunshine as she moved out the door.

This was also the signal for the rest of us to move into the kitchen of the gathering house to carry the dinner out for the humans. All hands were busy and the table was set and filled with food when Sunshine returned to the dining room and we reached for the hands of those next to us to thank the great network of caring souls who contributed to our meal: the farmer who grew the food, the people who picked the vegetables, those who carried the food to distribute among the shops, those whose hands had placed the food on the shelves, those who had carried the food from the shops, who had cut and sliced and mixed and boiled and roasted and baked, and finally for our Mother Lake whose water we would drink.

After which we fell to eating and chatting.

The lighting in the gathering house was just bright enough to make out one's neighbors. Oh, the lighting throughout the camp, if you can call it a camp, more like a haven, was always candlelit, making everything look soft and dreamy.

We sat around an oblong table, allowing an unobstructed view of one another's faces.

After settling into our seats, Keeya turned to me and gave me her name and explained where she had come from, and then added, "And you must be Whippoorwill. I understand you come from the United States. You must be very brave to have traveled on your own without knowing where you were going."

"Oh, but not so brave as you, traveling from Botswana," I answered.

"I am not so brave. My father had meetings in Zurich, and I asked to tag along."

"And your mother was okay with your leaving?"

Keeya paused a moment. "My mother is no longer one of the family consultants, you might say." She explained this with an easy smile.

"Oh, I understand," I answered. "A single parent household, they call it. I'm a product of one of those myself. It's just me and Louise making all the decisions." Then, returning to the subject of courage, "Though it must have taken some guts to leave your father and come here."

"As much as it must have taken you to leave your mother."

"Yes, maybe we are both more intrepid than we think. I'm not sure, though I am a Willingly, and Willinglys are meant to be quite plucky when it comes to travel. Who knows if I would have agreed to this adventure if the man who approached me about the trip weren't so kind and if I hadn't dreamed of the Mother Lake the night before he spoke to me about coming here. But, daring or not, look at us. We are here, in this amazing place, on our own. Now that I have arrived here, I feel perfectly, resoundingly courageous."

"Yes, I know what you are saying," answered Keeya. "I only arrived yesterday and feel like the bravest of the brave ones. Perhaps it's the lake that gives us such courage."

"I wouldn't put anything past the powers of that lake," I said. After which we settled into our meal and the conversation turned from many into one. There was talk of the horses, and how much they were appreciated by the group of travelers. There was, of course, conversation about the lake, and the mystical appeal that seemed to charm us all into such a deep sense of contented happiness.

At some point I asked, "Who owns this place?"

Everyone stopped talking and appeared to think about the question. Some smiled quizzically, as if the question had never occurred to them; others looked as if the thought had risen in their minds at some point but had never been voiced. Finally it was Mayan who laughed and broke the spell. Laughter was always very close to where Mayan was. "The lake?" he suggested.

"That is good enough for me," I answered. "But who is it that runs the place? Who organizes everything?"

"Oh, that is easy to answer," said Sunshine. "The Bright Ones." At the mention of this, everyone smiled warmly.

"And who are the Bright Ones?" I asked.

"Those who watch over us and guide us. Those who help us to use our gifts," answered Sunshine.

"I would almost think you were speaking of angels," I said, half joking.

"I do speak of angels, but the word is almost too small," Sunshine spoke, as if to herself.

"Or perhaps too distant?" added an older man across the table, speaking in a strong Scottish brogue. I had taken particular notice of this man during the singing. He looked to be in his seventies, with a great long, gray beard. I had noticed at our singing time that this man had stood next to what I now know to be a highland sheep. He wore an expression of perfect tranquility mixed with wisdom. He seemed a man who one would hope to have as a father or a grandfather or, better yet, a teacher.

"Do you mean that you believe in angels?" I asked the man, curious and somewhat excited to meet an adult, especially a man, I must admit, who might accept this concept as a possibility. As I mentioned above, my mother had spoken to me often of the idea of the angelic kingdom when I was younger, and I had eagerly embraced these beings in those early years, calling on them often for help. But I had outgrown the notion, and in the last year or so had come to completely dismiss the concept of invisible helpers. In truth, I had become a little sarcastic and had come to view the existence of such heavenly aid as childish, like calling on the tooth fairy.

"This is one of those rare places, Whippoorwill," said the man, "where belief is not required." And at this statement the others smiled.

"I don't entirely understand."

"Belief requires a good deal of patience, doesn't it? You were likely willing to believe many magical things when you were younger, and naturally some of these beliefs will have faded over the years, such as the belief that a jolly man in a red suit will squeeze down your chimney on Christmas Eve to deliver presents. The Mother Lake is a place of rejuvenation of some of your early beliefs, those founded on truth, that is, such as that of intervening aid from above."

"But what exactly is an angel?" I asked this man.

"All descriptions fall short, I'm afraid, because words, though quite useful in most cases, could never do justice to them," the man explained. "But perhaps a glimmer would suffice to educate you?"

As he said this last bit, he looked slightly above himself, with a questioning gaze.

It was at this point that I was gifted with my first unmistakable experience of these forces of light. Subtle at first, a gentle luminosity entered the room from above. As if a pitcher filled with faint starlight was being emptied onto us, the radiance spilled down, at first lighting our hair, then brightening our faces, moving onto our shoulders and down our arms. As it spilled, it grew in intensity, setting everything aglow, the faces of my companions, the food on our plates, the water in our glasses. Everything looked as if it were lit from within, and all the faces around the table took on an expression of such ecstasy, as if pure gladness had washed everything, every past criticism, every difficulty away. I found I couldn't begin to locate a moment in my past which was anything but joyful, as if I had led a completely charmed life, and had never doubted this light. I sat marveling in the sheer enchantment of this experience when the light reached and spilled into my heart. Oh, and this was the most extraordinary sensation. I thought I might explode with the intensity of tenderness. It was as if every thought was replaced with a gratitude so powerful that, like a tidal wave, it had washed all skepticism from my heart. As if every defect in my character had been replaced with love.

I looked at Keeya and saw that she was softly crying, and so were most of us, though Mayan was grinning happily and clapping his hands. Sunshine was looking up into the lofted ceiling with such a look of joy that she looked to be the same age as her beautiful son. I am not sure how long we sat in this tremendous state of elation before the light began to dissipate, and the room returned to its candlelight glow.

Our party let out a sort of unified sigh and rested in silence before I felt the need to comment.

"Oh me, oh my," I gasped and, thinking of a phrase that my mother was fond of, said, "I think the rules on planet earth just changed."

6

I woke to birdsong. A chorus of birds, large and small, serenaded me as I turned to look out over the lake. Our lake wore the morning light like a bright blue puffy-clouded dress. There was a little door in my bedroom leading to a small private garden which reached down to the path that ran along the shore. It had been too dark to make out the details of this garden the evening before, and I couldn't wait to see what was growing there. Sebastian, as if sensing my spirit's return from the land of dreams, trotted in from the sitting room and rested his great chin on the side of my bed. I reached to give him a good rustling of the head and watched the beautiful Lady Lake play with her early morning reflections. The Mother was in a particularly spirited mood this morning.

Finally rising from the bed, I splashed my face and mouth with water, which was all that was required to feel completely refreshed, and thought back to the nice man at the conference assuring me that all would be provided. I couldn't have guessed that it would be a lake that would offer so much of what was required.

"Good morning!" a friendly little voice called from the garden behind my cabin. I ran to the small door to open it. There stood Keeya and her lovely antelope. Keeya held a small tray in her hands with breakfast dishes. Pearl, at the sound of our voices, came racing around the corner of the little cabin to greet us with her joyful braying. I moved to hug Pearl in greeting, and then turned to Keeya.

"Today is my day of service," Keeya announced, looking very proud.

"Do you mean to say that this tray is for me?" I asked.

"Every bit of it," she answered.

"Oh, it all looks so delicious."

On the tray sat a steaming cup of something that smelled of sweet apples and cinnamon, accompanied by several buttery, flakey baked goods which gave off the scent of wild honey and ripe berries. My mouth fairly watered.

"I will leave you soon to wake up on your own," said Keeya, resting the tray on a little table next to a low chair.

"Oh, there's no need for that. I wake up when my eyes open."

Keeya laughed and added, "I have several breakfast trays to deliver, or I would love to stay and talk. But your day will be filled with interest." She reached around her back to remove a small backpack, out of which she pulled a bag of rolled oats for Pearl and a covered dish with Sebastian's food; I will not say dog food because Sebastian really wasn't just a dog, as I have mentioned. Both animals stood statue still in anticipation of their breakfast as Keeya unpacked the goodies.

"I hope you slept well," Keeya said to me, placing the food on the ground for Pearl and Sebastian.

"I must have, I don't remember a thing. Oh, except…" Something came bubbling up in my mind. "Does the Mother Lake ever speak to you at night?" I asked. "Or rather put thoughts in your mind to ponder?"

"I believe she might, yes," answered Keeya.

"I woke up wondering if I might not want to be a little more careful of how I speak of certain classmates of mine. It wasn't a reprimand, she wasn't upset with me, it was more of a suggestion, something to consider. I believe I did some thinking overnight. You know, I'm not so good at thinking on my own, though I am an only child, and am sometimes on my own for whole bits of time, but I do not seek out silence, and tend to think out loud."

Keeya smiled, quietly listening.

"My mother, Louise, is a very fine listener," I went on. "She says it is a skill one has to learn in the Willingly family. That's my last name, Willingly. The Willinglys are particularly verbose. That's a word my mother uses. She says that not every moment has to be filled with words, that sometimes words clutter up the landscape of the mind, or something like that. I noticed that last night Sunshine and I were able to walk through the forest in perfect silence, perfect silence! It was totally delicious! I have to try to remember how we did that. I really have to try to remember exactly how we did that."

Keeya began to laugh, such a gentle, stifled, giggly laugh. She tried to hold it back but there was no stopping this laugh.

And when I understood that she might be laughing at me and my wordiness, it struck me as being so comical that I began to laugh. And then she laughed a bit harder, and I laughed even harder, and began to snort. Tears began to fill Keeya's eyes. The animals began dashing around, pretending to charge one another, the antelope hopping and running around, Pearl bucking and braying, Sebastian chasing them both.

"Holy tomatoes! It's a laugh party!" I hollered. And all of a sudden, all five of us exploded with full-blown happiness. Tossing away all restraint, we chased each other through and around the trees, laughing, as happy as the tip-top happy number on all happiness meters. A pack of crazy happy tomatoes.

We kept this up for a bit before finally coming to rest and collapsing on the ground, all five of us.

"Whew," I said, "I hope we didn't use up all the happiness for the day."

"Impossible," Keeya said, rising and brushing herself off. Looking over at her antelope, she offered the challenge. "I'll race you to the kitchen, you old cantaloupe." And off they shot, leaping through the forest, with Keeya doing a very good job at keeping up with her nimble lechwe.

I pulled myself up from the ground and drank the delicious hot cider, and nibbled on the food, sharing some bits with Sebastian and Pearl. It was all so satisfying.

What came next was an experience that illustrated that some things are best studied in silence. The full appreciation of a garden, for instance, requires a degree of stillness and focus. I know that this might surprise you, but I hadn't yet learned the names of all the flowers. Of course, the flowers do not know their names, and I presume they don't much care whether we learn them or not, except that it might cause us to focus our attention on them more completely, and I have come to believe that everything on earth responds to loving attention. Everything: humans, animals, fish, trees, mountains, lakes, everything!

This was mid-August, and many of the flowers had already shown their colors for the season, but those that were still blooming were exquisite. After circling the garden several times very slowly, I lay on my belly, chin resting on my folded hands, and practiced noticing, and then I noticed for a little while longer, and after that, I put in a bit more time noticing. I was so still that the birds were willing to come very near to me, almost landing on me several times. I was so motionless that Sebastian and Pearl fell fast asleep, sprawled out in the little yard, both gently breathing. The sun was now spilling onto the garden, warming all of us: animals, plants, me. I remained unmoving, absorbed with the little chorus of flowers, until something remarkable occurred.

I would swear that the flowers put on a little show for me. When I thought but did not speak the thought—I know this is hard to believe, but I was learning the skill of wordless communication—I looked at a flower and merely thought the words, "You are the most beautiful flower I have ever beheld in my entire life," I had the distinct impression that the flower responded. It grew more intensely colorful, more velvety, more sweet-scented, more alive. The flower appeared to thrill at my enjoyment. There was no mistaking this. I could sense that observation, mixed with delight, held a power of which I hadn't previously been aware. It seemed to cause the flower to be more alive than before. I could see this happen. When I say this, I mean that I could actually see the flower glowing with life. Once I saw this in one flower, I experimented by moving my attention to the flowers surrounding the original. I scootched over on my belly and focused my attention on another flower and another, and it appeared that as each flower was effected by my interest, each came more alive. I was conducting a study in the potency of focused delight.

I vowed that day never to forget this moment,

and making a pledge to myself I whispered, "When I grow up, I promise to have a garden and fill it to the brim with praise."

I am not sure how long I was at my flower studies before I felt someone staring at me. I turned on my side and looked over my shoulder. Sebastian and Pearl had both raised their heads as well to look out in the direction of the lake. And there he stood, the black faced, white-wooled, highland ram from the night before, the one who seemed to be connected to the gentle, older man who had sat across from me. The sheep stood watching me with such a curious expression. We locked eyes for a moment.

"Good morning," I greeted him. He blinked, nodded, and trotted off, sure-footed, moving along the shore of the lake. "I wonder what gift that one represents?" I said, perhaps to Sebastian and Pearl, perhaps to myself. And then, clearly to myself, "Maybe it's time for me to get dressed."

In my bedroom there was a wardrobe with a simple array of clothes: my evening outfit, which I had carefully hung back up the night before; a day outfit which was similar to my evening attire but with shorts and a simple tunic shirt; pajamas, which I had remained in since I woke; and a bathing suit, implying that swimming might be on the schedule. Having no idea what I would do next, I slipped on the bathing suit and pulled the day clothes on over it. Prepared for the best, I reasoned.

There are several sounds a horse will make that I will always associate with that week. The pleasurable sounds of horses always make me smile. I heard one such sound just outside in the garden and ran to the door to see who was there. Two horses stood watching the back door of my little home, one of which had a human aboard. It was Sunshine on a dear little bay with a heart-shaped star on her head. Cowslip stood next to her, nickering her greeting.

"Hello you beautiful creatures!" I called, and Cowslip moved to position herself next to a chair in the garden, inviting me to climb up on her. I ran to do so, scrambling up onto her back, feeling her warmth beneath me. I hugged her from above, burying my face in her sweetgrass scent. If you have never buried your nose in the neck of a horse, you must, dear reader, you simply must. Again, there was no bridle, no saddle for either horse, and

Sunshine and I sat comfortably atop the strong backs of our gentle friends.

"I have already had such a beautiful morning; I can't imagine holding all of this happiness inside of me. I might burst with it," I said to Sunshine as we began to move along toward the path that circled the lake. "I had a laugh party with Keeya, a noticing party with the garden, and now a ride with you and Cowslip and…" I waited for her to tell me the name of her horse.

"Primrose," Sunshine answered.

"Oh, I like that name."

"All of the horses are named for the alpine flowers found in these mountains," she explained.

"Ah, beautiful," I answered, and then with a glad shout, "Good morning, Primrose!"

Primrose continued on with her peaceful pace, as I turned to see what Pearl and Sebastian were up to, worried that I was leaving them behind. I needn't have fretted, for there they were, trotting behind us, no doubt with full knowledge of where we were headed.

"I will be your guide today, Whippoorwill," announced Sunshine, "though that isn't precisely how it works in these parts. However, I am to be with you today as your companion."

"Oh, lucky me, then," I answered, and added, "I promise not to bombard you with questions, I do promise this. You know, I can be so full of words sometimes that I miss my surroundings. I just had the most extraordinary experience of silent examination with my little garden and its charming little gathering of flowers, and I swore to myself that I would remain quiet, almost circumspect (if you know that word), so that I won't miss anything, anything. I really plan on not missing anything." And then taking a breath, "Oh, dear."

Again, the laughter rose up in me and was mirrored in my companions. Sunshine was laughing, and the horses suddenly broke into a trot. Sensing that this was a bit bouncy for the humans they were carrying, they kindly moved into a canter (a very comfortable gait), and we rode as if gently flying along the path. Aloft, we glided along, as Rembrandt might travel this very trail. I could feel the rush of wind filling my lungs with dew-washed air—it was delicious. We rode like this for some time, the horses putting out little effort, Pearl and Sebastian loping just behind, moving effortlessly as well. We rode on and on and a bit farther on, until I noticed that I had been riding at a canter with absolutely no fear, not even an ounce of concern. "My, my," I said, "this is just perfectly delectable!"

Finally we came back to a trot and a walk, and the horses began to descend the slope down from the path to the shore of the lake. But surprisingly, they did not stop at the edge of the lake for a drink, as I had assumed, but walked right into the water, with the surface of the lake coming midway up their legs. Yet still they did not stop, and the water rose to their bellies, then past their bellies. All of this coincided with my feet dipping into the water, then my knees, my middle, and finally my whole self, which eventually found itself floating above Cowslip's back. I took a big chunk of her mane in my hands and moved along with her as she continued swimming out toward the middle of the lake, moving as easily as a leaf might float on the surface of a stream. I turned to look at Sunshine, who was gliding effortlessly next to Primrose. Pearl and Sebastian came paddling up behind us, Pearl looking particularly pleased with herself.

I am not sure how long we swam that morning.

Occasionally I let go of Cowslip and floated around on my own, with all the animals circling and occasionally blowing water out of their noses. Sunshine would let loose her grip on Primrose as well and swim gracefully along with the animals. We swam and swam and then swam some more, until I lost all sense of how long we had been in the water. We swam for sheer joy, sometimes rolling on our backs, we humans, to float in the sun. We swam yet more, until I had to wonder whether anyone could spend such a long time swimming without tiring. And the oddest part was that I felt as if every minute in the lake was replenishing rather than depleting my energy. I was growing stronger and more confident, diving down and plowing through the deeper water and then popping up through the surface and up toward the sun. At one point it occurred to me that we might eventually have to make a decision to stop swimming because our bodies clearly were refusing to let us know that they wished to stop. The temperature was perfect, and we simply could not tire. It was Sebastian who finally turned for the shore and, as if a whistle had been blown for time out, we all dutifully followed.

Climbing out of the water and flopping down in

the sun, we all began to dry, and Sunshine and I to talk.

"Did you have any dreams last night, Whippoor-will?" Sunshine asked, ringing out her thick hair.

"I believe I must have. I woke up thinking about a girl in my class." And then, I'm not sure what caused me to suddenly shift in mood, but I felt the sharp edge of a memory break the surface of my mind, which brought with it a bit of irritation. "I don't know what's wrong with her. Sometimes she seems to like me and at other times she can be such an awful pill."

Sunshine chuckled to herself.

"A few weeks ago she was in one of her unfriendly moods and said to me, 'You know, Whippoorwill, everyone in the class thinks you talk too much.' I was mystified. 'Everyone?' I asked her. 'And does everyone get together and have meetings about me? And did they take a vote? And was it unanimous? Everyone thinks I talk too much?'" I snorted a bit, which caused Sunshine to cover a smile with her hand and clear her throat.

"And what was it that disturbed you most? The idea that they had been talking about you, or the idea that they think you talk too much?"

"That they were all talking about me, criticizing me," I answered.

"That does seem a hurtful thing to imply," replied Sunshine, adding, "whether it is true or not."

"Do you think it may not be true?" I asked

"Do I think it might be true that your classmates talk about one another, and sometimes what is said is not so complimentary? Sadly, yes. Do I think that this friend was exaggerating, or a had another reason for saying this? Likely. " She thought for a moment, and turned to me. "Tell me, do you ever talk about a classmate with another classmate? And perhaps not so kindly?"

"Hmph," I groaned, "I don't much care for this phase of personhood."

Sunshine laughed outright. "And were you given an impression in your dreams of what the Mother might have thought?"

"Mm," I answered, "I did feel Lady Lake trying to communicate with me. Maybe if I didn't talk so much, I could remember what she was trying to tell me." I was able to laugh a bit at this, but not too much. "Let me be quiet for a moment and think…" I said and did just that.

And then, as if the idea were given to me, I said, "I'm thinking that it is a good reminder never to speak for another, never to begin a sentence with, 'Everyone thinks,' or 'I'm not the only one who thinks…' It can be pretty mean."

"A wise conclusion, Whippoorwill."

Sunshine and I sat together in silence for a little while when I began to notice the light on the shore shift ever so subtly, and at the same time, felt what seemed to be a gentle hand on my head. Like my own mother's hand, yet lighter and more…well… otherworldly, if I might use that word. And for a second time since I had arrived, I was aware of what Sunshine had called the Bright Ones. Light was very gently spilling down onto our heads—I could see it glistening on Sunshine's rich black hair, and I could feel its sweet warmth on my own head. I thought about all the times that I had spoken badly of my classmates, of the times I had essentially called meetings to discuss the bad behavior of one of our friends. I thought I would like to give up such behavior, that I would like to begin at this moment, this very moment, to rid myself of this habit. And all the while the light spilled onto my head, enlivening me, encouraging me. When all of a sudden, another thought arrived, a not-so-friendly thought. And this thought I voiced. "But she started it," I said to Sunshine. "She attacked me fist."

And POP! POP went the light. POP went the warmth. POP went the blissful feeling. Sunshine and I sat staring at one another: I in amazement and she with a look of playful understanding.

"The Bright Ones are shy," she explained sympathetically. "Faultfinding chases them away."

"Oh, oh dear, oh dear!" I looked above me, around me. "Oh don't go away!" I begged. "Please, please, I'm so sorry!"

Sunshine smiled compassionately.

"Oh, have I really scared them away?" I asked her, feeling suddenly, utterly miserable. "This happened to me when the nice man, Humphry, was telling me about the travel arrangements. I boasted about my willingness to be adventurous, comparing myself to a friend who wasn't so brave, when everything faded. Oh no!" I moaned. "So I really chased them away?"

"Well, yes," Sunshine answered with compassion.

"Will they ever come back?" I pleaded, even more desperate.

"They always come back, Whippoorwill."

"Oh, I hope so!" I practically wailed.

"But you must make room for them."

"But how do I do that?"

"Well, it's a bit like sitting on a sofa: You have to move over for them."

"How so?" I was madly eager to understand.

"Simply by being generous—generous in your spirit."

"But I can't help but notice things, can I? I can't help taking notice of people's behavior?"

"Of course you will notice things. It's a good thing to be discerning. But can you allow that there might be a reason behind someone's behavior? Some criticism they might have suffered that led them to criticize you?"

"Yes, yes, I see. Oh, it's so difficult to grow up," I said, pounding my fist on the ground.

"I can certainly agree with that," Sunshine said with a stifled laugh.

"But you are a grown up. You've already done all of this hard work."

"I'm afraid it's a never-ending effort, this thing you call growing up. My classmates are now my friends, my family, and the family of man around the world. I have to remind myself to be more generous every day."

"Have you ever said anything to frighten the light beings away?"

"Oh, goodness, yes!" she answered emphatically, "They are highly sensitive, and we humans can be awfully forgetful of ourselves. Humans are quite imperfect."

We sat thinking about this for a moment, looking out over the lake.

"Mother Lake seems to love us, no matter how forgetful we can be," I suggested.

"Yes, you are right about that," Sunshine comforted. "Don't worry, Whippoorwill, it's impossible to chase the Bright Ones away for long. In fact, they have plans for us this very afternoon. They will return."

"Whew," I sputtered, and lay back to wait. "I won't say a word until the Bright Ones return."

7

OF COURSE I did not stick to this promise. It was Pearl who finally interrupted our conversation with the delivery of our lunch. We hadn't noticed that she had trotted off to fetch it. She returned trumpeting her bray. As joyful as the humans had seemed over the privilege of being of service to the community, Pearl seemed even more so. She walked up to us with a high stepping gait, as if serving royalty. She wore a light saddlebag across her back and bowed to us, rather formally. I leapt up to praise and hug her.

"What a fine creature you are, Pearl! How did you manage to slip away and return unnoticed? And what is this?!" I questioned, removing her saddlebag. "Such a surprise!" Searching through the saddlebag's contents, I found all sorts of treats: carrots and apples and some sort of oat muffins for the animals, and a couple of the most beautiful sandwiches that Sunshine and I agreed we had ever seen, brimming with deliciousness.

Hungry after our long swim, we tucked into our goodies. "There is something special in this sandwich, some sort of magical ingredient," I murmured, munching away.

Sunshine mumbled in agreement, absorbed in her delight of the meal. The animals, each intent on their treats, seemed to savor more than usual what they were eating.

"Can you tell me a little of what will happen this afternoon?" I asked Sunshine, lowering my sandwich to take a moment between bites.

"I do not know exactly what the Bright Ones have in mind. I presume that we might get to know a little more about what they are capable of doing for us—or what they're teaching us."

"Oh, that sounds intriguing."

"But we mustn't assume that everything we will encounter this week will be entirely happy making," Sunshine warned. "Informative, yes, but not, like our lovely swim, utterly joyous."

"You remind me of something that my mother will say: 'Don't forget, Whippoorwill, that we are still on Planet Earth; not everything is perfectly rosy.'"

"I like that mother of yours," Sunshine smiled.

At some point during lunch, we were interrupted by the arrival of Rembrandt. The wide-winged, moonfaced owl came in to circle us several times before he landed gently on the ground next to Sunshine.

"Dear Rembrandt," Sunshine said, reaching out to touch his feathery head. "Have you come to travel with us?" Rembrandt made one of his many happy sounds, a kind of whirring.

"Travel?" I asked.

"Don't worry, we will only move in spirit, and we will do so outside of time."

"Can we do that? Who does that?" I asked.

Sunshine smiled at this, saying simply, "We must trust the Bright Ones on this."

"Well, if I learn nothing from the week but to put my trust in the Bright Ones, I will have learned a good deal."

"Amen to that, Whippoorwill," laughed Sunshine, before searching the sky for signs of the Bright Ones. "I imagine they will be along soon."

"I'll keep my eyes peeled and hold the judgey thoughts," I said, finally able to laugh at myself a little. We waited for a bit together, humans and animals.

Suddenly seeing something out of the corner of my eye, I blurted, "What was that?"

"What?"

"Something small and yellow."

"I didn't see it," reported Sunshine.

"It looked like a kitten."

"Did it?" Sunshine looked around, curious. "Did you say it was yellow?"

"Yes," I answered before rising to my feet to follow the little thing with my eyes. "It's gone now. Oh, maybe it will come back. It was so small. I think it must need caring for."

"I imagine you will see it again," reassured Sunshine.

"Do you think so?"

"I am almost certain," she added mysteriously.

"Hm," I grunted, and settled back down on the ground, next to Pearl. "I have a cat," I said as I scratched the donkey's head.

"Tinkerbell," Sunshine offered.

"Does everyone in this country know everything about me? You don't have to answer that. If I followed every mystery in this place to its source, I wouldn't be able to move forward." And then I confessed, "Actually, Tinkerbell left the world two months ago."

"Yes…" answered Sunshine, adding further mystery to the mystery.

I paused, wondering whether in this case I should attempt to explore the roots of this mystical knowing, but decided to push on.

"The problem is," I went on, "I cannot seem to speak of her in the past tense. I suppose I must learn to do that at some point."

"Must you?" asked Sunshine, genuinely curious. "Do you still love her?"

"Madly and truly! She was my best friend."

"And can you imagine loving her any less?"

"No, never."

"Even if another kitty were to arrive in your life?"

"My love will never dim for Tinker," I said with firm resolve. "Oh, I know I could love another cat, if that is what you are asking. I could love that little yellow kitten. I could start loving that little darling this very day."

"Then your heart was opened by your love for Tinkerbell, and not shut over the sorrow of her loss. It's fairly impossible to bury a love that keeps living in us, isn't it? But hopefully that love will not keep us from loving again. Hopefully our hearts are always growing ever more roomy. Remember what we determined about the Bright Ones, and how they can more easily visit when we are generous of heart?"

"Yes, like scootching over on a couch, we make room for them."

"Perhaps your love for your Tinkerbell is already making room for the Bright Ones to bring you another such love."

"Oh, I hope so. I have a friend who tells me that she will never get another cat because it almost killed her to lose her last one."

And at this, the strangest thing happened. A look of such sadness came over Sunshine, something that I had guessed at the night before, when I first met her, but that I hadn't seen revealed fully. Like a cloud covering up our lake, for a moment

Sunshine seemed to lose her rich colors, as if the sunlight had dimmed around her. "Yes, that can happen," she said softly. "But I've been thinking… Perhaps the Bright Ones aren't so easily fooled by these pronouncements of ours, like that of your friend who tells you she will never be able to love another animal. Perhaps they know that they must be patient with us, give us all sorts of time. Loss can squeeze the heart so, causing it to almost petrify."

I watched Sunshine for a moment, not wanting to disturb her beautiful, solemn expression. I understand that this was highly unlike any previous behavior of mine, but the fact was, I waited in perfect silence, petting Pearl, who remained beside me. And, more unusual still, I was comfortable with the quiet. And then it happened, for a third time: I sensed the presence of the Bright Ones near us. Sunshine looked up from her reverie, lifting her arms straight above her head, hands open.

"You've come for us, dear ones," she said, with such joy in her voice. "I think we are ready." Turning to me she asked, "Are you ready to go on a little journey, Whippoorwill?"

"Oh indeedy-deed, I am. Holy cannoli!" And I reached my hands up just as Sunshine had done. "I'm all in!"

And then something quite unimaginable happened. I felt my hands go warm, as if they were being held by a pair of invisible hands, and I began to rise up. I was being gently lifted, up and up and out of my body, until I could see below me the figure of myself, resting, as if slumbering on the ground next to Pearl. But where was I if the body I was looking down on was me? My mind was entirely alive and awake, more awake than I believe I had ever felt—or have since felt—myself to be. I looked beneath me at Pearl, who sat watching over my body, as it lay down to take its restful nap on the ground next to her.

I could see the figure of Sunshine as well, eyes closed, lying back in the grass, with Sebastian near, and keeping watch. I searched for Rembrandt but could not spot him. The horses grazed calmly nearby.

Lifting my gaze to look around me, I could see Sunshine hanging in the sky nearby. She was radiant, with a sort of body, yes, but one that appeared to be made of both matter and captured light. She

shone. I wondered whether I shone as well. Before I knew it, Sunshine and I began to move up and off across the lake, slowly at first, but all the while picking up a bit more speed. We rose up and out of the valley, and continued to rise, over the tops of the trees, until we burst up and over the surrounding mountains.

This afforded us a view of even more mountains, a great wide landscape of mountains. Once we rose above the highest peak our pace increased even more. Soon we were moving at such a speed that the landscape below us became a blur. Land turned to sea, and back to land, and back to sea and back to land. I cannot say how long this period of travel took; it felt timeless and, at the same time, as the blink of an eye.

Eventually our pace slowed, and we began to descend toward the earth. Lower and lower we drew, until we could see a lush green landscape. A river valley ran through low hills, and a town had been built on either side of the river, connected by a bridge. The houses and buildings were painted bright with bold colors: blues, pinks, greens. Occasionally, what looked to be temples were scattered among the buildings, some rounded with domes, others like tiered spires, some brightly white-washed, others ancient in earth tones. We dropped lower, heading for a stand of trees along the river. There were people among the trees.

We dropped lower still and finally came to hover over a large group of people, perhaps five hundred in number, most of them dressed completely in white. Was this a wedding of some sort, I wondered? The closer we came, the better I could see the faces of those at the gathering. They did not look as if someone was marrying. This was clearly a somber occasion, though the group was outside in the sunlight and the beauty of a rich springlike landscape gleamed all around them. They stood in an unorganized circle, with their attention focused on a spot near the river where a great tree stood with an enormous canopy of green, shading nearly half the people in the gathering.

It was Sunshine, floating beside me, who broke the silence. "We wear white at funerals in our country."

And then I saw her beneath us, through the branches of the tree. A woman, holding a box of ashes, scattered handfuls of these ashes in the water, weeping and scattering. Bereft with grief, she threw these handfuls of ashes from her position under the great tree which, in contrast to the mood, was in full spring bloom, heavy with flowers. Standing next to her, clapsed to her knee, was a child, a toddler. Seemingly happy to have found that he was standing on his own, or almost on his own, he looked about, smiling broadly.

More than all the people surrounding these two souls, more than the five hundred or so gathered to participate in this rite, I saw the Bright Ones. I could see their forms now, human-like but with a moving, sparkling luminescence. Many of them were leaning over to hold the mourners at the gathering, and whispering in their ears, comforting them. Far outnumbering the people, the Bright Ones tucked themselves among those gathered, in some cases floating above them in a sort of protective ceiling of light. The Bright One nearest to the woman with the ashes seemed to almost envelop her, so much so that it appeared as if for a moment they were one bright being. Another Bright One knelt next to the child and tussled his hair, praising him for his ability to stand on his own. The child looked happily into the Bright One's face, and beamed with pleasure.

The emotions in the crowd washed through me like waves. I had no resistance to the reactions of those beneath me, no protective shell. Just as the Bright Ones were now exposed to my vision, I was exposed to the thoughts, collective and individual, of those gathered. Apart from the feelings of the mother, who I understood was mourning the death of her husband, I felt the distinct sympathy and deep sorrow of a particular man who stood on the periphery of the gathering. I was given to understand that he knew and cared deeply for the two under the tree. He had been a friend of the man who had died and knew the family well. His empathy was overwhelming to him, so much so that he could not have moved in any closer to the two mourners or he would have shattered from his grief, or so he believed. More, I seemed to comprehend everyone's beliefs and thoughts all at once. It would have been a cacophony of sound had the thoughts arrived as voiced words, but there was no sound at all. I simply knew what they were all thinking, as if the information had been shown to me by looking at a beautiful painted panorama of a complex landscape. Each thought a hill, or a flower or a tree. It was delivered to me in one sweeping moment of awareness. Many at this gathering were feeling utterly lost, as if thrown into a foreign city with no map and no language to find their way. They felt homeless. Who was this man who had died, I wondered? Why did the mourners feel so ungrounded by his death?

As we floated above, watching the scene, I discovered that if I chose to focus on one individual, I would comprehend their own personal panorama of thoughts. I chose to study the man whose tender sympathy seemed to paralyze him. His heart was grand and fragile and filled to the brim with sorrow. Unlike most of the mourners at this event, his thoughts were not focused on his loss, but on the loss of this man, his friend, to the mother and child. He was filled with compassion for the two survivors.

I looked over at Sunshine, floating next to me, to see if she might be having the same experience as I, though how I might be able to determine this, I could not tell. Yet I was given the understanding that she too was following the thoughts of this one man. She hovered in the sky, perfectly still, with a consuming focus. I don't think she took a breath. She listened, or as I suspected, read the same thoughts as I was reading.

And then, out of nowhere, a great owl appeared above the crowd. The man we were studying was the first to notice the bird. He lifted his head and seemed to marvel at the sudden appearance of the owl. He sensed it must be some sort of gift, some sign from the man whose ashes were being scattered. The owl flew around the tops of the heads of the gathering until one by one each person looked above them to watch the creature's flight. Finally the woman under the tree raised her head to notice. The rest of the crowd watched as the owl hovered above the woman, very near, only fifteen feet above her head, his wings working back and forth to keep him alight above her.

At the same time, I could understand every thought of every attendee. They seemed to be thinking as a group, for it is possible for a group of people to be consumed by the same thought. They had all come to the same conclusion: This must be the soul of the man who has died. And their thinking went a step further: This is a sign that his wife and child still belong to him, and he is claiming their spirits to be his forever! The woman stared above her in awe. The man on the edge of the crowd wept.

But I could see, I could clearly see, that the owl was not the man who had died—the owl was an owl, the owl was Rembrandt. And I understood that the Bright Ones had encouraged the bird to come and hover above the crowd. I could see that the Bright Ones had manipulated the owl to perform this show to lift the heart of the woman. It was meant to be a comfort to her, a gift from the Bright Ones.

After a moment, Rembrandt, growing restless, flew up and away across the sky. The woman knelt down to hug the child at her feet and whispered something in his ear. I could hear her, as clearly as if she were whispering in my own ear: "Your father's here, darling. We are his, his forever." The child then lifted his hand and laid it on his mother's cheek.

And all went black.

I AM not sure how long I slept on the ground next to Sunshine, but I woke as if from a deep nap. When my eyes opened, I found myself being studied by the thoughtful gaze of my precious Pearl. As eager as a mother over her sleeping child, she watched me. Sunshine continued to sleep nearby under the watchful attention of Sebastian. The lake shimmered in the late afternoon sun.

I rose and stretched, and Pearl did the same, shaking off her lethargy. Tiptoeing over to look at Sunshine, I could see that she was still in a deep slumber. Sebastian looked up at me, and I understood that he would keep watch over her until she woke.

"Sleep, Sunshine," I whispered. "Sleep with the Bright Ones." And I moved toward Cowslip, who very kindly positioned herself next to a log for me to easily climb up on her back.

We walked slowly back to the cabin in the late afternoon light, with Pearl moving along beside us. Wrapped in rare, thoughtful silence, I tried to make sense of the scene we had witnessed. I would have to be patient and wait for the pieces of this story to reveal themselves, and oddly, I felt uncharacteristically willing to do just that.

There are some stories that must be disclosed slowly, one step at a time, like taking a walk with someone we hope to understand better. If our friend's story is parsed out to us at a walking pace, we are able to see the landscape of their life as it unfolds, able to understand how they grew into the person they have become. I was learning to take life at a walk, much finer a pace than all of the dashing around I had indulged in during my short life on Earth.

"Let's walk together," I will say these days, when hoping to have a real conversation. "Let's walk together at a listening pace."

8

MY BATH that evening was full of thoughts of the happenings of the afternoon, as if I were being given a lesson in careful reflection. Not the sort that hastily sums up a situation, with all sorts of easy conclusions, dividing up and stuffing the various feelings in cubbyholes of clear understanding. Of course I knew who the mother was, who the child was, and now I knew a little of the man at the edge of the crowd, or so I believed, having read his thoughts, but their stories, their love stories (you might call them) were complex. The lake was helping me to see that this was not a fairy tale—this was the carefully woven story of three people, three individual souls, and that the Bright

Ones had never left their sides, had never stopped watching over them.

At some point during my bath, it became clear to me that there were hundreds of reasons why the Bright Ones had chosen to wait five years to show Sunshine the truth behind this scene of the scattering of her husband's ashes. And, though I could not begin to untangle all of those reasons, I could see a very clear purpose for allowing the man to think that he must never approach Sunshine with his love. Part of that reason had to do with this man's relationship with the deceased husband. I hoped to learn more about that.

That Sunshine was having a similar teaching in her bath was also apparent to me. I sometimes felt as if I were Sunshine, or sharing a piece of Sunshine's soul, as she took her bath in the Mother's water.

Keeya came to escort me to the gathering hall that evening, her gentle lechwe in tow. Pearl and the antelope walked ahead while Keeya and I followed, catching up on our day.

"I hope you had a nice day, Whippoorwill. Were you able to swim?" she asked.

"Oh boy, did we ever swim! Sunshine and I swam with the horses. It was tremendously exhilarating, and I hope it is on the schedule every day."

"I imagine that can be arranged," Keeya responded with a smile.

"And did you have a nice day?" I asked, not wishing to talk about what had come after our swim. It wasn't mine to tell.

"I spent the day doing what might be considered chores and had a boatload of fun," Keeya responded, and then adding the confession, "I'm not always such a happy soldier when it comes to chores at home, I must admit. Sometimes I'm an out-and-out sourpuss. My father could tell you about that."

I laughed. "Your father and my mother would have a lot to share. What is the secret to enjoying housework?"

"I will tell you," Keeya said as if sharing a magical secret. "The Bright Ones, if you ask for their help, make everything lighter, more appealing." And then, almost as an afterthought, "Oh, and I learned how to cook."

"All in one day?"

"Yes, I believe so. Though I suppose I may have

already forgotten some of the details. It seems to have everything to do with deciding to enjoy oneself and slowing down to do one thing at a time."

"Oh, that's interesting. Yesterday I would have guessed that you would have been given all sorts of shortcuts, ways of making the chore of cooking go faster, but today I am thinking a little differently." And turning to Keeya, "I believe that might be the same recipe I learned this morning for enjoying a garden."

"I imagine it could be the same," she said, "looking at each flower, one at a time."

"Precisely," I answered. "Well, I will look forward to my day to serve, then."

"Oh, but there's one more thing required for rewarding cooking—the final ingredient."

"And what is that?"

"Love."

"Love?"

"Yes, you need to ask for love to be added to what you are cooking. Asking that love be added to the food you are preparing is the final step. Or perhaps the first step. It's magic; it works."

"And did you make the sandwiches today? The ones Pearl brought to us?"

"Yes. Did you feel the magic?"

"Indeedy-deed, Sunshine and I both did. They were awesome." Turning to Keeya, I performed the ridiculous gesture of offering a high five. *Slap!* went our hands. This silliness caused us both to wish to run, and we took off like antelopes.

Running through the forest in the low light of evening was another bit of magic that I could enjoy with Keeya. More than anyone I have ever met, Keeya loves to run for the pure joy of running. This place was a perfect place for Keeya and her antelope to tear through the trees, leaping over fallen branches, darting around stumps and rocks. I would follow behind at more of a fierce trot, with Pearl doing the same. Keeya was two years older, possibly two feet taller (or so she seemed), and easily twice as fast as I was. But there could be no competition in this place, only pure enjoyment. Her love of running was infectious.

We were nearing the gathering hut at top speed when we heard the singing. We slowed our pace to a walk, and finally came to a complete halt. Pearl, after a brief fit of enthusiastic braying, grew silent, while the rest of us caught our breath until finally we were all able to hear over our slowing breath.

The scene was precious: night falling over our beautiful lake, the golden glow of candlelight playing through the windows, the hauntingly gorgeous sounds of harmony, the animals joining with their unique squawks and murmurings.

We all crept quietly into the gathering room, tucking ourselves into and among the group to join in with the singing. Keeya's gentle steps (steps that I was to learn were taught to all school children in Botswana) made us all move as one, gently pacing out the steady rhythm of the song. Mayan and Sunshine were there already, holding down their parts, and holding each other's hands. Sunshine looked as I had never seen her. A simple, naturally pretty woman, she appeared radiantly lovely that evening. Or perhaps I should say she radiated her individual gift of beauty. It seemed to me as if all of Sunshine's beauty had been released, like a flock of doves into the sky, beauty that had been caged for many years.

My mother told me the story of seeing a friend she had not seen for some time, and when she did see her, this friend looked entirely different, as if all the seeds of her beauty that had been growing all along had suddenly blossomed at once. She asked her friend what had been going on in her life, and the friend confessed that she had fallen in love.

Sunshine could not have hidden her miracle of love had she been covered in a shroud of black. She sparkled. I could hardly keep from staring at her.

At the end of the singing, Keeya announced the feeding of the animals, causing the nightly haywire heehaw among the beasts, as the humans moved to set the table and carry in the meal.

Once seated, I found myself between Mayan and a young woman who I was to discover was from Peru. Her name was Estrellita, and she looked to be in her late twenties. I had noticed the animal that had stood—or, to be precise, rolled around at the feet of this young woman—and learned from Estrellita that he was a giant river otter. Apparently, she told me, the otter could not stop himself from playing in our Mother Lake. He played all day and was only able to settle back on land with the rest of us in the evenings. When Estrellita spoke of the lake, she was clearly as in love with it as was her animal companion. She confessed that she had spent the better part of the day cavorting with her friend and told me with wonder that she never seemed to tire, not all day.

"Oh, I can believe you," I concurred. "Sunshine and I and the horses swam for hours this morning, and I felt as if I could have gone on for days. Sebastian had to persuade us to come into shore."

"Sebastian is a wise creature," Estrellita agreed.

At which point she was asked a question from George who sat to the other side of her, and I turned to my right to speak with Mayan.

"Did you have a nice day, Mayan?"

"The best day ever," he answered. "I went for a long ride into the mountains on Wolfsbane. Do you know him?"

"I don't."

"He is the elder of the horses, with a thick and uneven coat, long mane, great bushy tail. He is as tall as a house, or so he seems to me. My feet never touched the grass as we traveled through the fields, as they had when I was on top of Cowslip."

"Were you alone?"

Mayan laughed a bit at this. "I had Wolfsbane for company, and Ruby following. But if you mean, did I have human companionship, the answer is yes. We rode with George, who preferred to walk, and of course he walked with his highland sheep."

"Oh," I answered with a touch of envy. "I hope I have a chance to speak with George someday."

"You certainly will, you can count on that. George is our grandfather."

"Your grandfather?"

"Our grandfather. All of us here. You don't have

to understand," Mayan kindly comforted. "But you can rest assured that you will have time with everyone who is here this week. We were brought here at the same time because we are related to one another, but not as we usually think of being related; not by blood, but by…" (He searched for the words) "…a sort of gravity of the heart."

"Hm…" I responded, liking the way that sounded. "I'm not going to ask you to clarify but will just sit with the magic of that phrase for a bit. Heart gravity…" I repeated the phrase, and added, "I no longer try to figure everything out that I witness here but assume the answers will come when it's timely that they do."

"That sounds like a good plan," encouraged Mayan.

"I'm working on slowing down my thinking so that I can learn more," I told him.

"You are better at this than you think, Whippoorwill. Just look at how you enjoyed your garden this morning."

"But how do you know this?" I looked at Mayan in wonder.

"Oh, dear, I know I can be unnerving to some people." He looked a bit troubled.

"Oh, I'm not unnerved…" I began to say.

"I'm not shown everything, you know. The Bright Ones hold some things back from me."

"You can speak with them?" I asked, eager to hear more.

"The short answer is yes. I used to think everyone could speak with them."

"Is this your gift, Mayan?"

"I suppose it is," he answered, as if only now realizing it. "And maybe that is why Ruby is my companion." He thought some more.

"And what does she represent?"

"Black leopards are rare in India. There are very few sightings these days. Maybe they are a bit like me. I understand there are only a few people who can speak directly to the Bright Ones. Is this true, Whippoorwill? Are there really only a few of us who can communicate with them?" He looked troubled, and an expression of concern overcame his otherwise bright face.

"Oh, but maybe there are more people than we think, Mayan. Maybe they are shy to speak of it. Not everyone would understand."

Mayan continued to wear a pensive look.

"My mother, Louise, would believe you," I said.

"She used to tell me about angels all the time, until recently, after I grew a bit…" And now I was searching for a word. "Cynical?"

"I don't know that word," said Mayan, turning to me for help.

"It means when you want to appear more grown up than you are, and pretend not to need anything, especially help from above, as they call it. It means you might have lost something precious."

"I think I understand, but maybe I'm not grown up enough to have gotten there."

"I'm pretty sure you will never be that grown up, Mayan," I said, confident in my prediction.

"You know," he confided, "not everything that I see is happy, Whippoorwill."

"Yes, well, that makes sense. My mother will say that happiness is overrated. Not laughter, she always reminds me, laughter is a necessity. People laugh hardest at funerals, she tells me." And then I remembered the vision from the afternoon, of Mayan as a toddler, looking in the face of the Bright One, as he clung to his weeping mother's knees. His face had been so beautiful. "You seem like the happiest kid in the world, from the little I know of you."

"I have some friends who make me laugh," said Mayan, smiling.

"That's a big, hefty blessing, isn't it?" I answered. "We're not going to grow up entirely and stop laughing, are we? I've seen some grownups who don't appear to laugh anymore. It's pretty frightening."

"No, that will never happen to us," said Mayan, with a fake gloomy look on his face, followed by his familiar cackle.

"Happiness is one thing, dependent on everything lining up just so, but laughter…" I paused to ponder. "Laughter can happen in a high-winds stink storm."

And at this, Mayan and I began to chuckle, and then laugh, and then we began to choke with laughter, until it became obvious that we were helpless in our inability to stop laughing, and finally, the only thing left to do, after the snorting began, was to politely excuse ourselves and step into the kitchen.

It was a perfect ending to a stunning day.

9

I WOKE TO the strangest of noises coming from the side of my bed, a low guttural sound. Frozen in place with my back to the sound, I tried to imagine what might be behind me. A dragon, I wondered? I had learned not to discount the appearance of anything in this astonishing place.

Slowly turning my body to face whoever it was that was behind me, I found myself looking into the yellow eyes of a great black cat, whose rumbling growl now shook the bed. I am not sure how long I held my breath, but certainly as long as I could physically do so, before I heard faraway laughter. Ruby moved from her intense assessment of my face to look out toward the lake, allowing me the freedom to breathe and follow her gaze. Mayan sat in a little rowboat just offshore, waving and beckoning for me to come and join him.

Sebastian was the next to arrive in my room, leaping on the bed and nudging my back. And right on cue, Pearl dashed around the side of the cabin and into the garden to push her great head through the doorframe. I never did figure out who it was who had opened that door.

I wonder whether you have observed, dear reader, something of a regular phenomenon among all house pets and some farm animals. I mentioned previously the habit existing in my cat Tinkerbell, that when my spirit returned to consciousness in the morning, she would react as if the landing of a plane had just been announced, and race to my bed to watch my arrival into the new day. At times an animal will react before the landing, or the arrival of their owner's car in the driveway. They can anticipate the arrival and show up for the excitement. Pearl and Sebastian always knew when I would be waking.

Clearly it was time to get up. Leaping from my bed, I ran to splash my face with lake water, threw on some clothes, and skipped out to join Mayan. All the animals followed. When we reached the lake, we could see that Mayan sat in the little rowboat with a breakfast tray next to him, with enough on it for two human animals, and a couple of four-legged ones. It was all so enticing: the morning, the little meal, the prospect of breakfasting while we floated around on the surface of the Mother Lake. But though Sebastian and Ruby could accompany us, I worried about Pearl.

"Oh, dear, Pearl, I don't think this little boat will be able to carry you. And, even if we could squeeze you in, I fear the boat would make you very nervous with its tippy-ness."

I needn't have worried, as the moment I said this, George walked by, carrying a walking stick, and followed by his highland ram. George, though in his seventies, I would guess, still walked like a thirty-year-old.

"What a grand sight to see this morning," George said, pulling on his long gray beard and smiling. "Are you off to the island?"

"Good morning, George!" answered Mayan. "Would you like to join us?"

"I was rather hoping Pearl might wish to join me and Curdie on land," George said, offering, "Come, Pearl, we have a beautiful walk in the hills planned for the day. You and Curdie can test your climbing skills."

Pearl seemed overjoyed at the prospect, braying with delight as she trotted over to join her climbing companions.

Satisfied that Pearl would be entertained for the day, I thanked George while Sebastian and I

climbed aboard. We pulled away from the shore with Mayan rowing. Sitting low in the boat, I watched the slight ripple from the boat's oars as we moved through the water on this perfectly windless morning. The surface of the lake was mirror-like, showing us her deep sky pictures.

Feeling reflective myself, I thought of Pearl and the chances of George arriving with such precise timing to take her for a walk. "Solutions seem to turn up in this place without delay," I said to Mayan. "It's like magic. I wish it worked that way at home."

"Do you?" asked Mayan, and then thought for a moment. "I wonder whether we would be as grateful for the solution at home if it arrived like clockwork."

"Oh, you are likely right, Mayan. I'm sure we wouldn't be as grateful." And then, after a pause, I added, "You little wiseacre."

This was the first of many laughs we had that day.

After we had rowed for a bit, we stopped to float in the middle of the lake and eat our breakfast. There was plenty for the four of us, and we all sat enjoying our meals. With the sun just high enough to warm us, we rocked ever so slightly in the Mother's arms.

"Tell me about where we are going?" I asked, breaking the still morning spell.

"We're headed to the Island of Memories."

"Oh, that sounds enchanting." I thought about what an island of memories could mean. "Well, depending on the memories, I presume."

"The island will accept any memory, even the most difficult. In fact, it has never refused a memory," Mayan said.

"I don't think I understand. Is it a place where something horrible happened? Was someone murdered? Or was a bloody battle fought there?"

"All of that, you could say, and more. But nothing is left of these things; it is as clean as the sky today," Mayan assured me.

I looked at the sky, cloudless, clear as polished glass. "How do you know how clear the sky is, Mayan?"

"I am not always sure how to answer that question. I learn things about the world, about my surroundings, in different ways. I just seem to know. Today, I just know that the sky is perfectly blue, without a cloud. It's as much of a mystery to me as it's likely to be to you." Mayan rested back, thoughtful for a moment before he added, "Last night my mother became as cloudless as the sky is today. I wonder whether you noticed?"

"I did notice a difference in her, yes," I answered.

"I wonder what might have chased the clouds away?" Mayan said, thinking aloud. "This place has its mysteries, and if nothing but this happy change comes about in my mother, it will have been well worth the journey."

"Maybe it's the Mother Lake that causes all of this mystery. She is certainly a power."

"She is that," Mayan agreed, and we fell back into quiet.

You might be wondering, dear reader, why I did not bring up the vision of the day before, and the man, and the thinking around the appearance of the owl. There were times during my visit to this place when I felt very strongly that the Bright Ones wished for me to remain quiet. Keeping my mouth still, as I have mentioned too many times to count at this point, had never been one of my strong points, but I felt I was making some little headway with the skill.

It was Mayan who brought up the man in the vision.

"We have a friend, a man who I have known all my life. There is no one who can make us laugh harder than this friend. Once he made my mother laugh so hard that juice shot out of her nose. I was only about four years old when that happened, and I remember being so happy as I felt the juice misting down on my head. My mother hadn't laughed much before this. In fact, laughter was all but missing from our home. She was like the sky all covered with gray clouds. Her light, though keeping us alive, was dim and a little stingy in the way that a day without any sunlight can seem. The chill had crept into our home and made us both feel tired. After the juice shot out of my mother's nose, I believed the sun had a chance at shining through the clouds. The clouds were still there, but there was a bit more warmth getting through. I call this friend who made my mother laugh Uncle Bookshop. I call him uncle not because he is really an uncle, but because I wish he were a member of our family, and I call him Bookshop because he reads to me and has even translated a few books into braille for me. He knew that I would like them, you see. He is the kindest man I know, besides George."

There was so much I could have said, yet still I remained circumspect.

"George is a writer, did you know?" Mayan said.

"No, I didn't know. I so look forward to having some time with him."

"That will come," Mayan assured me, as he had the night before.

"What sorts of things does he write? Does he write for kids or adults?"

"Both. He writes for all of us."

"What do you mean by all of us? Everyone in the world?"

"Would that this were true. No, I mean all of us here."

"At the Mother Lake, you mean?"

"Yes, and many more. For a couple of centuries."

This was one of those moments during my week at the Mother Lake where all I could do was pause and wait to see whether the mystery around such a preposterous statement as the one Mayan had just delivered would be revealed, or whether I should trust that it would be exposed in time. I was just trying to make up my mind whether I should ask for an explanation when a face, a very dear and comical face, poked itself up from the lake. It was slick and brown with a nose covered in long whis-kers. It had shot up and out of the water directly beside the boat to peer deeply into my eyes, and at the same moment, the joyful sounds of laugher could be heard behind the boat.

"Come and swim with us!" shouted Estrellita. "The Mother is in a playful mood today!"

Before any of us had time to second guess the invitation, we were in the water, all of us, includ-ing Ruby, who swam with the grace of a swan, head skimming the still surface. We didn't have to worry about the boat floating away, as there wasn't a puff of wind. When we were all in the water, the otter shot away from us and dove and flipped and popped up and out and back under the water. He did this again and again, spiraling, splashing, skimming, floating on his side, on his back, on his belly. He tried out every move as if he had never explored it before, relishing his movement through the water. His love of swimming was infectious, with each of us catching the swimming bug with wild abandon. Sebastian chased Ruby, Ruby chased the otter, Mayan chased them all.

At some point I became caught up in a series of backward somersaults that seemed to possess me with a furious joy, after which I raised my head to discover Estrellita mesmerized by the production of a spiraling corkscrew movement, which she was practicing with unbridled delight. This fascination with swimming was all-consuming and so happy-making that I couldn't imagine ever stopping, as every move seemed to bring more energy, more appeal. This was as joyful as the swim the day before but multiplied ten times. Joy on joy on joy! We might have swum for hours like this, it was difficult to tell, as nothing we did in the water seemed to exhaust us in the least. Mayan might have swum five miles that morning, chasing Sebastian and Ruby, and I believe that I might have executed five hundred summersaults and Estrellita a thousand corkscrews. Astounding delight!

It might have been the otter who eventually began to corral us, or perhaps it was Estrellita, but each of us finally fell in sync, with the six of us slowing our frantic pace to form a wide circle. We paddled placidly around and around in silence like this before Estrellita broke the quiet. She did so by beginning to sing, gently at first, and finally leading us to join her in a sweet and simple song. It was a round with three parts and a song that I was to learn later was from an area in Peru in the rainforest, along the Madre de Dios river, (another body of water, I realize now, which is recognized as a mother). The song's lyrics were in a language that none of us knew, not even Estrellita, and we were to learn later that this was one of the seventy-some languages spoken in Peru. This ability we had to sing in another language was another mystery, my friends, and one that I apologize I never came to understand. We took up our parts, we humans, as if we had been singing this song since early childhood, with the animals barking and growling and chirping along with us.

We formed a chorus in the middle of the lake and sang our hearts out. Or, perhaps I should say, we sang our hearts full. We might have sung and paddled like this for an hour or so and, I was later to learn from Estrellita, we sang in at least six different native languages of her country. And, as we sang (and this is another mystery, dear reader), I saw, in my mind's eye, the landscape of Estrellita's beloved country: the Andes Mountains, the sultry rainforest, Lake Titicaca, the bright still deserts, and dense cloud forests. I saw these landscapes in both their sweeping grandiosity and in their tiny details. I saw butterflies that I could never have imagined, pumas, macaws, over one hundred varieties of hummingbirds, pink dolphins, sloths. I saw huge fig trees, tiny flowers and insects moving underneath thick, dense leaves of the forests. These visions, along with what I understood to be Estrellita's exuberant love of her country, caused me that day to make a solemn vow not only to visit Peru when I was grown but to do everything in my power to hold this grandly diverse beauty in my memory. It seemed a palace full of unopened gifts, discoveries that I knew I would someday unwrap and hold.

I know now that this was the day when I became an environmentalist. If this seems sudden, perhaps it might be understood by considering my interest in the squirrels that I had so carefully studied in New York. I understand that the word "environmentalist" can mean many things, and I pray someday that all people will be environmentalists, but my vow went deep. I knew that I must study and work in the field of planet restoration, an idea that would have seemed absurd to me just moments before this vision. Up to this point, I hadn't seen much more than the carefully designed landscapes of Central Park. But, that day, I knew, without a doubt, that I would dedicate my energy to the preservation of this palace of gifts that has been given to us. I saw my path, and I knew, like my patient Pearl, that I would follow that path with plodding perseverance, and furthermore, I understood that I would be following in Estrellita's footsteps. I knew she would be my mentor. We were going to be part of saving the Earth. We were going to love the planet back into health together.

The sudden awakening to this clear direction caused me to make a wild backward flip and somersault and shoot off in an underwater dash for the boat. Mayan and our two animal companions followed, heads up, doggy paddling together, leaving Estrellita and her otter to float, belly up, sunning themselves in the still midday peace of our Mother Lake.

We clambered aboard and rowed our boat away from the two bobbing, sunning bodies, knowing that they had no intention of joining us but were determined to remain in the arms of the Mother until the late afternoon sun drove them in to shore.

Mayan took up his oars and we continued toward the Island of Memories.

10

MY MOTHER will tell anyone who asks that my father was fundamentally unable to fulfill his role as a parent. "Imagine," she would say, "that we are all actors in the large production called life, and we are cast in our various roles by… well, by someone who perhaps thinks more of us than we do of ourselves. This someone believes that, with time, most of us might be able to play even the most difficult of roles, that we could be brought up to the part, so to speak, with a little patience and hard work."

My mother would say, when I asked about my father, "He was just miscast, darling, he wasn't up to the job."

I understand now what she was saying. I had

been in plays in my years at school. I had watched kids struggle with certain roles. But, at the time when my mother first raised this theory with me, I still held the belief that, if my father knew me, he would see how easy I was, how breezy it would be to be my parent, and he would jump into his part with both feet. I continued to believe this until one day when I was five years old.

My mother and I were visiting the Central Park petting zoo, as we did most weekends, and were standing by our ancient, patient donkey, watching her greet every child and adult who came to visit her. I was well incarnated at the time. By that I mean, I had developed my powers of memory, and can remember that day quite vividly. When it came my time to visit with our donkey, we indulged in a good, long scratching session together, with the donkey leaning against my hands, twisting her head to satisfy every deep itch while wiggling her upper lip in satisfaction, when I turned to my mother to see if she was enjoying the donkey's expression as much as I was. She was as pale as milk.

"Are you okay?" I asked, looking around us to see if there was some receptacle of some sort where my mother might be sick, a trash can perhaps. But all I could see was a man holding a toddler in his arms and staring at my mother.

"Well, well, well, you never know what you're going to find in a petting zoo," the man said, and laughed. He had a rather silly laugh, a bit too giggly.

My mother's face remained still and bloodless.

"So this must be the offspring," he continued. "She looks like you. That's a good thing, I suppose. You were always the prettier half." He looked me up and down. "Well, she could stand to trim down a bit," he said, and then addressed me. "Be careful what she feeds you. If you take after your mother, you could blow up like an air mattress someday."

My mother's face suddenly sharpened from overwhelm to determination.

"Whippoorwill, this is the man who might have been your father, had he remained living with me during my pregnancy with you. And the weight gain, to which he has so eloquently alluded, is one of his excuses for his departure. Or so he chose to report upon his leave-taking." And turning to the man: "Whippoorwill is five years old now. She is quite grown up, and understands that mothers, when they are growing a child inside their bellies, will often gain extra weight to feed the growing baby. And she understands that the hope is that the baby will grow and grow into an adult eventually. Today she is being given a fine example of someone who looks to be grown but has yet to become an adult."

She then turned to me and touched me on my head and smiled. "Remember what I told you about the play, darling, about certain roles being difficult for some people?"

"Yes," I assured her. And turning to the man I asked, "Is that your baby?"

"It is," the man replied. "At least I think it is." And then added, "What day is today?"

"Why do you ask?" my mother questioned.

"Well, if this is the second Saturday of the month, this is my child." He chuckled to himself. "If it were any other day, I would have to say, no, not really."

"I see," My mother responded.

The toddler, unaware of the content of the conversation, reached his little arms out toward the donkey and bleated out an indistinguishable word. I stepped aside to allow the man and the child to draw nearer to the donkey.

As he stepped forward, my mother and I caught each other's eyes and took a few steps away from the scene.

"Careful of the donkey's eyes," my mother warned. "She is more patient with the undeveloped ones than she should be." She then took my hand and off we walked.

It was this memory that I carried to the island that day.

When we arrived at the island we stepped out of the boat and onto the shore to discover a well-wooded bit of land with a narrow footpath leading into its heart. After pulling the boat above the waterline, we set out to walk the little trail, with Mayan leading and Ruby striding at his side. Sebastian and I followed in silence. The place seemed to demand quiet, like a library. There was such a deep pile of pine needles that it might have been gathering there for centuries without breaking down in the least. The effect was one of perfect stillness—even the birds were silent. There are several types of silence. Some are awkward, like that at a dinner table after someone says something uncomfortable. Some are ominous, like the ones just before a tornado is about to touch down. Some are beautiful and full of anticipation, like the ones before sunrise, or the one that day on the island of memories. The farther we moved into the center of the island, the dreamier we grew, and the sleepier. Even the animals stumbled a bit and dragged their feet. Sebastian's head hung down, his eyes barely open.

We had walked for perhaps twenty or thirty minutes before we came to see the roof of a small structure and, as we neared, it revealed itself to be a sort of gazebo with two hammocks hanging from its roof, the sight of which made me impossibly drowsy, so much so that it was all I could do to climb the stairs to the gazebo and throw myself into the nearest of these hammocks. Mayan did the same into the other, while Sebastian and Ruby collapsed onto the floor. In seconds we were all sound asleep.

Have you ever woken from a deep nap and suspected that someone might have come along and pinned you down with leaden weights, ironed you onto the place where you lay, and filled your body with cement? Some naps are more like generation-long epics. You wake an entirely different person. That is, if you can bring yourself to wake at

all. I would guess that it took my eyes, the only thing that I could immediately imagine moving, a good fifteen minutes to open, and the rest of my body a good half an hour. But once I did awaken fully, and found myself standing next to my hammock, I was brand-new. Feeling as light as a cloud, I was full to the brim with eager expectation. I couldn't wait to get back to life. "I've had a life-ectomy," I announced to Mayan. "I've swallowed a look-forward pill," adding "I've drunk from the waters of yippee!" At which point, I believe I might have clicked my heels in the air.

The rest of the group looked like fresh-squeezed gladness themselves.

Mayan answered, leaping off the porch. "Let's race each other back to the boat," and shot down the path like a deer.

I never worried about Mayan and whether he might not be able to maneuver his way through his surroundings. He seemed better adapted to life on the planet than anyone I had ever met. He was at home wherever he found himself. The rest of us tore after him in pure exhilaration. Reaching the shore in a quarter of the time it took to reach our hammocks, we all pushed the boat out into the water and hopped aboard. Turning to the island, we blew kisses of thanks to whatever spirit, blessing, magical powers had caused us to feel so sparkly clean and zippy, and waved our hands in the air in salute. The animals chimed in with their growling and barking.

I rowed the boat home that day. Mayan chatted away, dipping his hand in the water of the Mother Lake as the animals craned over the side of the boat to spot fish. Sebastian made happy little whining noises at every sighting.

There were a handful of moments, of the briefest length, when a flash of understanding of what I left behind on the island would arise in my mind. As I mentioned, it was the story of meeting my father in Central Park that I had brought with me to the island. And it was that story that I was encouraged to both leave behind and view as a gift. I could see that I had lived up to that moment under the illusion that there might be something missing from my and my mother's lives, a hole that I suspected at the time might have existed by not having a husband and father around. It was this perceived hole that had been stitched together on the island. It was a mending of sorts.

Pearl was waiting patiently on the shore in front of my cabin as we returned, clearly on the lookout for us. The highland sheep stood next to her, but when he saw that our boat was nearing the shore, he must have understood that his donkey friend would have company, for he trotted off in the direction of the rest of the cabins.

My animal friends' anticipation of my return has, over the years, always been something that has caused in me both joy and a tinge of guilt. After I disembarked and was standing on the shore, I held Pearl for a good long while, scratching her behind her ears, staring into her deep eyes, squeezing her cheeks as I did so. "I hope you had a beautiful day, as beautiful as ours was," adding, "You are so familiar to me, Pearl, as if I have known you all my life." And to Mayan, "I knew another donkey when I was younger. She lived in the petting zoo in Central Park in Manhattan. She was an ancient beast with a gray muzzle and deep sunken caverns above her round, patient eyes. She was a grand spirit of a donkey. All wise and gentle."

Mayan smiled. "May I sit with you in your garden and tell you a story?"

"Of course," I responded, and once we were settled, he began.

"Two years ago my mother and I were invited to visit a cousin in the country. He was a great loner and lived far away from any neighbors, far into the wilderness, a wilderness relative to India, that is. This man must have felt sorry for my mother, she being a widow and a mother of a blind child. Therefore, very much against his nature, he opened his doors for us to spend a weekend with him at his house in the county. The first night in this place, while I slept in a room on the ground floor, I woke from a dream I was having of a great leopard who walked just outside the window of the room where I slept. I could feel her tremendous power, and her intention to make a kill, to find food for her cubs which she had left behind, sleeping. I understood that if I had been asleep on the other side of the wall that separated us, she might have decided to kill me, as she was hungry and so were the two young cubs. I couldn't go back to sleep for some time, thinking of this magnificent beast and her sheer power. I so wished she would return so that I might know more about her.

"The next morning, I told our host about my dream, and my belief that this leopard might have actually been outside my window in the night. I sensed it was more than a dream, that it was more of an awareness. Our cousin was very interested in my story. 'I have heard lately of a black leopard in the area, a female. The sighting of one of these leopards is very rare, almost mythical. In your dream, did you see her color? Was she black? Or was she the more common mottled brown?'

"I thought about the dream and answered, 'She was ruby red.'"

Again, dear reader, I did not ask any questions, I had to take this in. I looked at Ruby, I looked at Pearl. I looked at both of them again.

Mayan stood and stretched. "Well, I'd better be off to our cabin to get ready for supper," and added, "Thank you for joining me today, Whippoorwill, it was the best day of my life…so far." And then he and Ruby moved down the path, with Mayan's hand resting on Ruby's great shoulders.

I turned to Pearl. "I don't know what this place is. I don't know who you are. I don't know who Mayan is. I don't know who this great Mother Lake is. I don't know who Sebastian is. I only know that

I was born to love you all." And then, studying Pearl for a moment, I asked her, "Do you suppose this is what Mayan refers to as the gravitational pull of the heart?"

Pearl's eyes were as deep as the deepest sea.

11

THERE WAS a newcomer that evening for dinner. He was somewhere in his early thirties, English and with a round and jovial face. Indeed his face was so lovable that it seemed to make everything he said comical. He sat between Keeya and me and told us stories. He was a wonderful storyteller. His anecdotes of meeting the mysterious man with the gentle face, whose name I now knew to be Humphry, were more fantastic than anyone else's tales. His train ride was more harrowing, with introductions to every single passenger onboard. His horse ride was filled with the utmost adventure. He was followed by three foxes, five wild turkeys, eight goats, and a herd of cows. He attempted a headstand on his horse (fortunately it was Hawk's Beard, the draft horse), but it didn't go so well. He swam in the stream, met a turtle who at one point nestled onto the top of his head, and generally yucked it up from the moment he opened his early morning eyes until we met for the evening's singalong which, in honor of our new friend's arrival, was filled with comical songs and a rather ridiculous dance step.

His bath in the Mother Lake was taken in the lake herself, and his response to her therapy was utter exuberance.

His name, he told us, was Percival, but, he added, if we found that a difficult name to maneuver, he would answer to the name Lunch Box, a name, apparently, his school chums had given him.

At some point in his recounting of his day, Estrellita went from laughing to snorting and finally to a case of hiccups that caused her to have to leave the room and move into the kitchen. I thought to myself, *Well, if the purpose of life is to laugh as hard as you can, Percival is certainly giving us all purpose.* Estrellita made several attempts to return to the table but was shot out of her chair in helpless explosions of mirth and had to return to the kitchen.

When Keeya asked Percival where he had been when he got the call to come here, he answered, "I was watching the pinched and scarlet face of my father as he moaned through a hatha yoga class. We had come to a rather spare retreat center called… What was it called? Of course it was an Italian name, meaning something like Camp Shakedown or some such thing. I had taken the liberty to sign my father up for a week. The patriarch is in politics, bless him, and his nerves are a ripe beehive of agitation. He hasn't taken a deep breath in a decade." Percival went on, "Though I must say, I wasn't sure that this yoga class was quite the perfect ticket to relaxation. None of the attendees looked terribly happy to be there, apart from a man and a woman in the back row, and I suspect romance for their lighthearted attitude toward what was clearly a set of agonistic poses of wretched contortion.

"We were just moving from the neck-breaker to the spine-snapper when a man's face appeared at the door, a gentle, slightly nervous face. Attached to this face, by the neck, was a tall, slightly awkward body whose long-fingered hand seemed to raise itself on its own, as if on a puppet string, with the slightest of movements, and crooked one of those fingers in my direction. I was thrilled to leave the rest of my classmates behind to soldier on through the merciless bootcamp without me, and so I skipped out the door to see what this man might want of me." Percival paused a moment.

"But then," he continued, "I am sure you all know Humphry by now and understand what he wanted of me. He outlined the plan, and of course I said, 'You've got to be kidding. Leave this lower dungeon torture club and go tripping off to the mountains? Sign me up!'

"Later that night I sat at dinner with the patriarch and the couple of lovebirds whom I made mention of from the class—apparently, they had just met one another, and it was going swimmingly. 'It seems I've been called away to the mountains,' I said to them. 'And I simply must go. I won't be long. You'll be all right without me, Padre? I am off to, as far as I can surmise, a sort of supernatural dude ranch. And it sounds like heaps of entertainment.' At which point both the man and the woman seemed to come to attention. Up to this point, you might say, they only had eyes for one another. It was the woman who spoke first. 'And are you to bring nothing? Not even a second pair of shoes?'

'Precisely,' I answered.

And then the man asked, 'And does this place have a lake? A Mother Lake?'

'I believe it does, yes,' I answered.

'And is there a girl there? A girl with an antelope?' asked the man.

'That I don't know.'

'And is there another girl, slightly younger, with a donkey?' the woman asked.

'I'm not sure of that either,' I answered. 'Why do you ask?'

The woman answered, "We've been dreaming of them, every night.'

And then the man added, 'They've become friends; they run through the woods together.'"

Keeya and I looked at one another.

It was I who spoke next: "Does this woman have a great pile of hair on her head?"

"A very distinctive head of hair, yes," answered Percival.

And then Keeya spoke. "And does this man have legs as long as rivers, legs a bit like mine, only older?" She stood up, with her grand, long running legs, like straight, strong saplings.

"There is a keen likeness, yes," answered Percival.

Keeya and I caught each other's eyes and exploded into joy. We laughed until tears came down our faces. We howled, and then we took off. We ran outside and into the moonlight. We ran and ran, until we heard other feet, and saw that Pearl and the antelope were also running, running, and running for sheer joy. We might have run for hours. We never tired. We ran and whooped with gladness, all four us, until we could run no more.

It wasn't until my eyes opened the next morning that I thought to wonder what Percival's animal companion might be. I hadn't noticed any new beasts at the singalong. It was only moments after coming awake when the undeniable truth of what that animal was broke through in answer. The sound of the beast's call had been likened to a trumpet. But, depending on its proximity to one's bedroom, it could be compared to five hundred trumpets blowing all at once.

I leapt from the bed and dashed to the door, with Sebastian suddenly appearing at my side and

Pearl rounding the corner and into the garden. There we could see, on the edge of the lake, the cause of this sound. Percival stood knee deep in the Mother Lake while his companion sucked up great draughts of water through her trunk and drenched her human friend with blasts of spray.

"Come and have a shower, Whippoorwill!" Percival shouted, and my companions and I were off like bees to a sunlit garden.

Her name, I was to learn, was Mary, and her delight in washing us each down with her great fountains of water from the Mother Lake was absolute. Though I would estimate that her delight was multiplied tenfold by her little herd of humans and beasts which, due to her joyful trumpeting, grew in number until almost all of us in the group were lined up for our morning wash: Sunshine, Mayan, Keeya, Estrellita, Percival, and me, with our various beasts. Even Rembrandt suffered the humiliation of a good spraying. Eventually, the horses came down from the mountain and gathered around. After a good deal of shying and squealing and nosing forward and bolting they grew brave enough to attempt to come into the water. It was Primrose who was the first to stand still enough for a good shower. She trembled with joy, reared up, landed, and shot off into the hills. One by one the rest of the horses took their turns and then dashed after Primrose up into the hills where I understand they all had a fine roll in the deep grass.

They say that one bad apple can spoil the whole bunch, but it is equally true that one good apple, one exuberantly alive apple can…now what is the opposite of spoil? Refresh? Yes, one joyful, playful, bright apple can refresh a nation of spoiled spirits. I have since seen this play out in the world. One writer, one book, one screenplay, one storyteller (and Percival was a born storyteller), one bright voice can lift a nation.

To say that Percival had a big personality might imply that he took up a little too much of the air in the room, that his voice was a little too loud, his gestures a little too grand. But this wasn't the case. It was his generosity that was so huge. He seemed to have enough room in his large heart for everyone and every animal and every moment of the day.

That morning, after a good long play, all of us piled into the communal kitchen to serve one another breakfast. All hands were busy making

coffee, tea, toast, cutting fruit. All of us fed the animals, piling heaps of hay up for Mary. My mother will say, "Many hands make light work."

As we were seeing to Mary's meal, I asked Percival what connection he might have with elephants, and he told me a story of a trip he had taken many years ago, again with his father, to South Africa.

"Always the champion of equality and justice," Percival explained, "my father booked us on a trip to Johannesburg in the nineties. And, because he planned to be in meetings all day, he left me from early morning until late afternoon at an elephant reserve, just a short bush plane ride from the city. There was, of course, a herd of elephants there with a matriarch who was, interestingly, also called Mary. She was a very gentle creature that could be trusted to mingle with children. I spent many hours in her company. I believe she taught me more about tolerance and repairing wounded souls than I might have learned had I joined the meetings with my father, who was at that time involved in helping with the restoration of a wounded and divided nation. Have you ever watched an elephant herd, Whippoorwill?"

"Oh, good golly, no! I live on the concrete island of Manhattan. This is as far east as I have ever traveled. Though I am a Willingly, and Willinglys are known to travel. But I sooooooooooo want to travel to see the elephants!"

"You will adore them. There is such love and comedy in them."

"Did you say I *will* adore them?" I asked.

"Hmm?" Percival questioned.

"You used the word *will*. I *will* adore them."

"Hmm, yes, well, it doesn't take a prophet to predict what is in your future—yours and Keeya's."

"Oh my. I might have to do some thinking around this subject. I may have to stop talking for a while and do some thinking about this...but not now."

"Well, as you will. In the meantime, let's have a proper beach holiday, shall we?" Percival suggested. "Let's return to the shore. Back to the lake, friends!" announced Percival. "Our mother calls!"

We spent the entire day in and out of the lake, only breaking for lunch, which was also precipitated by Percival, allowing us to understand why his schoolmates had come up with the nickname Lunch Box for him.

We swam and leapt into boats, and leapt out of boats, we rowed and sang. Percival taught us a song that a friend of his wrote in second grade about warts. It was brilliant, all about the little crusty eyesores that rhyme with shorts. I still sing it.

At various times throughout the day, George would travel through our gathering in a little rowboat and one of the group would join him for a private chat. I hoped to have a moment to talk to him.

My time finally came, and I climbed aboard.

"Whippoorwill, how nice to have a moment with you," said George, smiling with great familiarity, as if we were old, old friends, or as if he were a dear, beloved uncle who had been missing his regular visits with me. "How are you doing this week, my dear?"

"I love this good place, these dear friends, these creatures, this lake more than I ever thought it possible to love so many things all at once."

George continued to smile. "And do you have anything on your mind today?"

"Well, yes, funny you should ask. I'd been waiting for a moment to reflect a bit." Taking my time, I formed my question. "Do you think I am going to have a new father?"

George took a moment before he answered, and he answered with another question: "Do you feel as if you need a father?"

I took a good while to think about the question before finally responding. "No."

"Then I suspect you will find yourself with a grand new friend." George smiled.

"But I could still use some direction, some advice occasionally. I don't want to lose my way."

"I wouldn't fret about that," George assured me. "We might lose ourselves, but we are never really lost. You rely more on your inner compass than you might think. And when that is difficult to read, the Bright Ones are there to help."

"Can you tell me more about the Bright Ones?" I asked him.

"I can only suggest you trust in their help."

"But how do I ask for their help?"

"Just ask."

"But who do I ask, who is it I am addressing?"

"I can tell you who I address, but a name will never satisfy all that the name hopes to imply."

"What name do you use?"

"Father. The Father of Lights. But I was fortunate to have had a fine example of true fatherhood in my father on Earth. He was a wonderful man, both loving and wise. Clearly, many were not raised with this privilege. Some would rather use the image of a mother. And yet to some, I am sorry to say, this would be difficult as well. There was a writer in the mid-twentieth century who used the image of a great lion, both loving and fierce. Whatever image we choose to employ, we must resign ourselves to the understanding that the image cannot begin to encompass the enormity of love and wisdom that makes up the one to whom we are speaking. And there are some who do not speak at all but sit in quiet communion."

"Oh, I'll never be one of those," I assured him. "I like to talk."

George had a good laugh at this. "Well then, perhaps tonight, while bathing in the waters of our Mother Lake, you can have a good and lengthy conversation with…" He paused here and looked at me.

"Friend?" I offered. "Or maybe the great loving donkey in the sky?"

George smiled. "And what are the qualities of your donkey that you most admire, would you say?"

After thinking for some time, I answered, "Perfect patience with pokey-fingered children."

George laughed at this. "I will have to remember that metaphor."

"Oh, I don't want to ever leave this place," I moaned.

"Not many do at this point in the week. But you will be ready when the time comes. In fact, I predict you will feel eager to return to life. You have such a lot of living yet to do."

"Hmm…" I answered, thoughtful. "Who is the choir, George?"

"All of us," he answered.

"You mean those of us who sing every night?"

"Yes, and more. All of us here, all of those who brought us here, all of those we passed along the way. All of those who we will pass along our path through life." And he continued. "This is a place where we are brought together with those we wished to connect with during our time here on the earth. This is where we have the chance to meet the small choir of vital voices of our lives. They are our handful."

"Handful?" I repeated, hoping for clarification.

"Yes, most of us have just a handful of souls, perhaps five (as is the case with you), who will influence and accompany them along their journeys. These people, this handful, will typically arrive at varying times in our lives. They each hold the ability to influence us, to send us in the best direction for our lives. But here, in this special place, we are allowed to meet them all at once. They are the original handful that will lead to more and more introductions. They seem to understand which seeds in your spirit need to grow, and they help those seeds to find good soil, so to speak, so that your life might blossom with goodness." George let this information soak into my thinking before continuing.

"The songs sung here teach us to be in harmony with one another. This is a blessing, but there is more to this singing than meets the ears. The songs, sung in such harmony, can, and do, ripple out. They ripple and ripple and wrap around the world. This is where the idea of the Choir is seeded. The Choir, if understood and seen completely, already reaches around the globe and encompasses every single soul. The Choir, the great earth's choir of souls, if we could hear it properly, if we could hear its song, would astound us for its beauty in harmony. But our ears are not yet developed to hear this. We continue to hear the chaos of the world. One day that will change—when we all learn to love one another."

"Oh, dear," I groaned. "You're talking about peace, aren't you? World peace. But that will never happen, will it? There's always a war going on somewhere."

"So far," George answered. "But there have been wiser and greater thinkers than either you or I who have believed that this world holds the potential to be an all-loving place and that the seeds have long ago been planted for this harvest."

And, as I had suspected when I first met George and could see that he was willing to believe in the concept of guiding angels, the idea of a world of perfect peace seemed possible coming from him. There are some people who have this ability to anchor the good beliefs of those around them. I have since read books, met people whose light seemed to shine for the rest of us, all of us whose little flames need the oxygen of another, stronger belief. George had this ability to share his hope with others.

When I grew to be a young woman, I began by

reading one, and then another, and finally most of George's writings. I have adopted him as my grandfather and continue to rely on his writings today. I hope, dear reader, that you will find at least one writer who you can trust in print. I hope that one of your handful of souls may be a writer whose books will buoy you up when your heart threatens to sink.

"I want so badly to believe in what you are saying," I assured George. "I hope your ideas of peace on this planet will someday come true."

"Perhaps that's all that is required of you today, my dear," George smiled, "a willingness to believe."

"I'll give you that," I answered.

"Then off you go."

"Thank you," I said to him, reaching my hands up to the sky. "Thank you from the bottoms of my feet to the tips of my fingers." At which point I dove off the little boat to join my handful of new friends, splashing, cavorting, spinning, laughing, as happy as the happiest soul given the happiest day the Earth could provide.

That night, when I tucked into bed, I thought about how warm and hopey I felt from my conversation with George. I thought if I needed a book to read (which I really didn't, being so sleepy from swimming all day), I would pick a book that was packed with hope, or at least one that pointed to hopeful things. I've since learned that I sleep better when I put something in my mind that has a good helping of hope in it before I fall asleep. If I don't, and I make the mistake of reading something gloomy and doomed, my dreams will be affected, filled mainly with nonsense and chaos. I don't wish to imply that I don't read sad things or hard things. These writings can still have hope in them. "Every shadow points to the sun," my mother will say, quoting Ralph Waldo Emerson.

I slept that night under a blanket of hope.

12

I WOKE VERY slowly the next morning, not wishing to leave the dream I was having. It was an ordinary dream, nothing fantastic, in which I had my arms wrapped around my departed cat, Tinkerbell. We were talking to one another. Of course, that last part was extraordinary, the talking part, but it wasn't so in the context of the dream. She was telling me how happy she was, and I was genuinely pleased to hear it. "I am very glad for you, Tinker, but I sure do miss having you around. I miss being able to hold you."

"I understand, Whippoorwill," she purred. "Perhaps it's time you accept a little gift that I have found for you?"

"It isn't a mouse, is it?" I asked, teasing her.

"No, something much sweeter. Perhaps you'd like to play the guessing game."

"Okay… Is it bigger than a bread box?" I asked.

"Do people use bread boxes anymore?" she countered.

"I'm not sure," I answered, and continued. "Can I take it to Africa with me?"

"I believe so, yes," Tinker assured me.

"Will the gift make it easier to leave this sweet place? I never want to leave this sweet place."

"Again, I believe so, yes." She purred.

"When can I have it?" I asked.

"This day."

It was after Tinkerbell made this bold pronouncement that I woke, wondering what sort of gift the day might bring. Every day at the Mother Lake, every moment, was a gift. I could not imagine what more I could be given. And, to illustrate the point, not a minute passed before I heard the bright voice of Estrellita calling from the garden. "Holla, Weep-poor-wheel!!"

I hopped out of bed and ran to the door to the garden. Estrellita carried a tray and rested it on the little table in the backyard. Her lovely otter sat next to her, rather calmly for an otter, I will add.

The morning's arrival of Sebastian and Pearl came next. Around the corner barreled the donkey, and from the sitting room and through the bedroom door burst Sebastian.

"Can you stay and talk for a moment, or do you have others to wake?" I asked Estrellita.

"You are my final stop," she assured me.

And, though there were a couple of simple chairs and a table in the garden, Estrellita folded herself, cross-legged, on the grass next to the flower garden. I joined her, happy to be nearer the scents of the early morning grasses and opening flowers. We shared the breakfast she had brought and at the same time shared some of what we loved about our time at the lake.

"I want to hear what your animal might mean for you," I asked, curious. "I'm hoping to write a diary of my time here when I get home. Do you have some connection to otters? Any story you might share?"

"Yes, I do have a connection to the giant otter. They are found in my country, in small numbers, and they are quite difficult to spot. You have to travel into the deep forest for many days, and you must locate the perfect habitat and then wait and

wait for a sighting. I live in a country that has pre-
served a good amount of land for its indigenous
people and wildlife. There is a park surrounding
the Madre de Dios river, for instance, that is as
big as the entire country of Switzerland. There are
giant otters found there, and I have traveled there
many times to try and see them."

"And were you able to see them?"

"Not until the third time I visited this park.
Not until I had given up on seeing a giant otter
altogether. On the final day of my third trip I was
gifted a sighting. During the last hour of the last
day, an otter raised his head right next to the boat.
I believe he came to give me hope."

"How so?"

"I was born to love this planet, Whippoorwill.
I rejoice daily in her beauty. I ache for her, bleed
for her when she is wounded, pray for her always.
I love her in sickness and in health. The giant
otter's recovering numbers in South America are
a hopeful sign of the planet's recovering health. I
was looking for a sign that I should enter a university in environmental studies. I am not sure why I
needed a sign. I was so sure of my love, so sure that
I wanted my life to revolve around the mending of

the planet's health. Why is it that we need signs to tell us what we already know?"

"That is a very good question, Estrellita. I don't know."

"When I didn't have a sighting the first two times I visited the area where the otters live, my doubts were in a frenzy. Doubts are like nasty little monsters, aren't they? They will tear away at our confidence. I wanted to chase my doubts away, scatter them, so I continued to visit the lake where the giant otters were known to be. And finally, on this day, on this one beautiful day, the face of an otter rose up out of the lake and almost touched me with his whiskers. I cried for joy; I couldn't stop crying. I had my sign. The monsters of doubt vanished."

"I love that story," I told Estrellita, squeezing my hands together and beaming. "And are you working in the field now?"

"Yes, and I couldn't be more determined, more enthusiastic. I know I am traveling the path of my calling."

"Oh, how wonderful. I so hope such a clear path will appear for me that gives me that much passion."

"I think it already has, Whippoorwill," answered Estrellita, smiling.

And at that, her otter approached me. Slowly, carefully, he moved over to me and placed one paw on my knee, and then he did something extraordinary. He climbed up into my lap and curled himself up for a nap. Now it was my time to cry. Crying for joy is so much more fun than crying over a hurt. I had what they call "a good cry."

"Sometimes the sign arrives before the request for a sign is voiced," laughed Estrellita.

I sat almost breathless, afraid to move for fear I might disturb the shy creature now asleep in my lap. We stayed seated on the ground for a good while, discussing what Estrellita did in her field studies. She spoke of the natural wonders of South America, of the animals, the variety of habitat. Finally, after a good long chat, Estrellita looked toward the lake.

"Do you think it's time for little swim?"

"It might be, but I don't want to disturb him," I said, gently smoothing the coat of the otter with my hand.

At this Estrellita burst into cackles of laughter, the otter raised his head, and in the wink of an eye they had both leaped to their feet, after which they glanced at one another and shot off to tear down to the lake. I stood to watch them as they circled and shot, circled and shot forward, like two wild puppies on a romp.

"I wonder what else the Bright Ones have up their sleeves today?" I said aloud.

And, turning to Pearl, who stood very near to me, gazing at my face, I asked, "What would you like to do today, Pearl? I don't feel we've had enough time together."

The donkey cocked her head, wiggled her great ears, and turned toward the path that circled the lake.

"Would you like to take the path around the lake?"

Pearl nudged me firmly in the belly.

"Well, let me put on my shoes, and I'll be right with you."

When I returned to the garden, Pearl began to trot toward the path, and I followed.

Looking back for a moment, I could see that Sebastian preferred to remain seated in the sun, perhaps aware that Pearl and I needed some quiet time together.

But then, of course, I am never quiet for very long. We hadn't walked far before I began to chat with Pearl. "I'm not sure I've told you about a donkey that I used to know when I was younger. She was also a miniature donkey like yourself, which I understand is a breed that came from Sicily. Did you know that? Sicily is an island off the coast of the mainland of Italy."

Pearl politely turned to acknowledge me as I explained to her where her roots might be found. I continued.

"This donkey lived in a nearby park, called Central Park, on the island of Manhattan, in a place called the petting zoo. Which means that she had to put up with the untrained fingers of amateur children. But, oh, she was so patient, this lovely donkey. When my mother and I would visit this park to see our donkey friend, we would sing to her. I made up the little song when I was about four, and I would always sing it when it was my time to pet her. It was a silly song, really more of a strange hymn, about loving all animals. In fact, it was a fine song! What am I saying? My mother might have helped me with some of the lyrics. But,

when I sang it, our donkey friend would always perk her ears forward and wave her head up and down. This might have been because the hymn was most often punctuated by the offer of a peppermint, but I don't think so. By the end of her life, our donkey became so glad of the song that she would give us a great bray of appreciation when she heard it. If I can remember all of the words, I will sing it for you sometime, Pearl."

We walked together, Pearl and I, for most of that morning, and I told Pearl my life story. I told her about my beautiful mother, and my child father. I told her about my progressive school and my friends. I confessed that sometimes I hadn't been so patient with my friends, but that I hoped to be loaded with patience when I returned to them. I confessed, though I used to believe in the Bright Ones, at some point in the last several years I had grown cynical, explaining what that word meant. "That's when you aren't so grown up but try and pose as a grown up and pretend that you no longer believe in magic and miracles. It's when you start saying things like, 'It's okay to cheat every once in a while.' Grades matter, you know. Or 'A little white lie never hurt anyone.' It's when you lose something super special and replace it with something not so noble, something cheap."

Finally, after some time of walking and reporting on my life, I stopped and stared at the lovely donkey next to me.

She turned and watched me. "Do you believe in the Bright Ones, Pearl?" She continued to look at me with the gentlest eyes. "Do you think it would be too much to ask them for a sign? I understand that I have seen their light, that I have witnessed forms of light in the sky over India, and that I saw Mayan looking into the eyes of a light being during that vision. But maybe that was all just a dream and nothing really happened. I understand that I have experienced some pretty miraculous things since I have been here, things I never thought possible, but maybe there's an explanation for it all, a practical explanation. Maybe this place was an old zoo, and the people who run it are having fun with us. Maybe there's a logical reason for everything that has happened." I shrugged, feeling more than anything like a fool. "Maybe this is just a big hoax."

I have since come to recognize this sudden onset of crushing doubt, or as Estrellita called it, the visitation of the monsters of doubt. I understand that it can happen to the best of us and at the oddest of times. It's interesting that doubt might arrive at a time when you are feeling so very happy. Doubt doesn't seem to play by the rules. It can break into your mind like a robber, and steal all of your confidence, all at once, and all that's left is uncertainty. How could this happen so suddenly? And in this of all places?

"I think I would like an undeniable sign from the Bright Ones," I said to Pearl, adding, "Is this too much to ask? Are we allowed to ask for signs from the Bright Ones? Or are we supposed to pretend to have confidence when we don't feel confident? That can't be right, can it? It doesn't seem right to pose as something you are not."

Pearl continued to stare into my eyes.

"What are you supposed to do when your trust has been stolen?"

Pearl continued to focus on me with such kindness.

"…when your pockets are all empty of belief."

Pearl looked as if she would like to give me anything I needed to feel hopeful again.

"You know, your expression," I said to Pearl, with wonder, "really everything about you, is so similar to my friend from the petting zoo. I suppose that is because you are a miniature donkey, and all miniature donkeys look alike—all of them coming from the same parents in Sicily and all—but I have to say, if you just had a little more gray on your muzzle…" I didn't finish this sentence because the light around us was pulsing, twinkling. I looked around. It was subtle, this change in light, and I was still able to hold on to my doubts, but I had to make mention of it. "Do you see that shimmering light effect, Pearl?" The light continued to put on its gentle show while Pearl and I looked around us, taking it all in. It was as we were turning and looking about for the source of the glimmering light that I saw something. It was just there, to our right, visible out of the corner of my eye. A small yellow creature streaked from one bush to the next, paused, and streaked again. "It's the kitten!"

Pause, dash, pause, dash.

"Here, kitty, kitty, kitty!!" I called, crouching down on the ground. "Here kitty, kitty, kitty!"

My calling was clearly having the opposite effect from what I had wished. The kitten was too wild and shy to find any comfort in my voice. She dashed into a large brambly tangle of low branches. I crawled after her, calling and calling. "Please, kitty! Please trust me!" I crawled deeper into the brambles. "I want to help you!" I pleaded. "Pleeeeeease…" On hands and knees I begged. "Please, please, please…" Still no movement. I slumped to the ground.

The kitten was undoubtedly long gone by now. I sat for a while, instantly as empty of hope as I had been hopeful the moment I had I spotted her. I was on a rollercoaster of emotions. Feeling beaten again, all of the doubts rushed in and replaced the hope I had so recently held. The light flattened. It must have been my imagination, I thought. All of the wonder of this place had to have been in my imagination. Everything was colored in grays again. "Oh, Bright Ones, if you are there, please let me know."

Nothing happened. Nothing. I sighed and crawled out of the bushes, plopping on the ground. Laying back in the grass, I brooded.

And then something very subtle did happen. Something popped in my mind. The song that I used to sing to the donkey in the park came back to me. I remembered the words. And I began to sing.

> We love all the beasties in the beastie world.
> We treat all the beasties like the angels would.
> Though Earth gives the feasties to the beastie
> world,
> I have a sweetsie for my sweestie girl.
> Aaaaahhhhmen.

Suddenly Pearl seemed to break into song herself, braying, waving her head up and down, cocking her head and wiggling her lips. But how could this be? She pranced around, heeing and hawing, shaking her head. How could this be my donkey from the park—and yet with me in this place?

I sang the song again.

"We love all the beasties in the beastie world."

Pearl danced and hopped.

"We treat all the beasties as the angels would."
She shook her head wildly.

"Though Earth gives the feasties to the beastie world, I have a sweetsie for my sweetsie girl! Ahhhmennnnnn!!!

Pearl ran and ran and ran around in circles. Utterly jubilant!!

How could this be? I ran to her and hugged her sweet neck, her round belly. I cried for joy at our reunion. Crying for joy is quite a delicious privilege. Crying for joy can hit a reset switch in your spirit. It did so for me that day. But how could this be? How could this be?

"Oh, me, oh my oh, I am so pleased to know you for who you are, you dear patient donkey. Was your name Pearl all along? And we never knew it?"

I hummed the song and we hugged for quite a time. We had a festival of recognition and joy that day.

"Oh, you darling, darling creature!" I continued to say.

We were so taken with our recognition of one another that we hadn't noticed the little yellow being making her tentative movement out of the bushes. The kitten, as precious a sight as the feeling inside of me at that moment, sat staring at us from a safe distance. I spoke to her.

"Have you decided to join us, little one?"

The kitten remained sitting and staring.

"I would like to take care of you. I could feed you, give you a home."

I crouched down on the ground and reached my hand out. "I could be your friend; we could look after one another.

At this the kitten crept toward me, low to the ground. She moved with slow, careful steps. I kept encouraging her. "I'll give you a name, if you'd like."

And then, snap! There was a cracking of a branch near us. It might have been Pearl, shifting her feet, and the kitten leapt up and was off like an antelope.

"No, no!" I wailed, my emotions beginning to plummet again. "Come back!" I hollered after the tiny, frightened thing. But she was gone, I could tell, long gone.

"Oh, poo," I groaned. "Double poo-poo!" I moaned, flopping back down on the ground.

Pearl folded herself down next to me, leaning in to comfort me. I held her, brooding over my bad luck with the kitten. "I'm just a big loser today, Pearl." And then, after some reflection, "No, I am just massively ungrateful."

I understood that the whole day had been a miracle so far: the miracle of Pearl, the beautiful lake, my life's direction encouraged by the sign from the otter and Estrellita. I was also made aware of what complex creatures we all are, we humans. How could I feel a failure on this of all days, you might ask? How could I be thrown so low after being so high? The truth was, I sooooo wanted that kitten, and I couldn't see past the want.

Pearl and I sat together for a little while, silent, with one of us wearing a big mopey face, when the voice of Sunshine cut through the air.

"Are you two hungry for some lunch?"

Turning, I saw our lovely Sunshine riding her friend, Primrose, a saddlebag over the horse's withers, with Rembrandt flying above and landing in a tree above us. As usual, there was no saddle or bridal on Primrose. It would have seemed disrespectful to the horse not to trust that she knew the way. The horses at the Mother Lake always knew where the Bright Ones needed them to go.

The Bright Ones had certainly brought me the right person, and at the perfect moment. But then, this is what Bright Ones do.

13

Sunshine possesses the power to chase away the clouds of doubt. I have known her now for many years, and this ability has only blossomed as she grows in age. Some people, I have noticed, don't seem to grow as they age. Sunshine, however, has grown like a great shade tree, giving relief to all who know her. On this day she deftly parried all of my doubts.

"But Tinkerbell said that I was to have a gift today, and I chased that gift away!" I lamented.

"The day isn't over," she offered brightly.

"But I can't stay here all afternoon and evening."

"Perhaps it would be best to trust that whatever is meant for you will come to you?" Sunshine offered, adding, "If it is right for you."

"I'm feeling rather low on trust at the moment," I sighed.

"Well, I can certainly relate to that feeling. When my own trust levels are bottoming out, I ask the Bright Ones for help in raising them, knowing that I am quite helpless to raise them myself."

"Oh, but I did ask them. I asked for a sign," I protested.

"And did you snap your fingers and say, 'I'll take that now, if you don't mind, and make it speedy'?" Sunshine teased. "Sometimes it's best to leave a request in the hands of the Bright Ones for a time, let them work out the timing. We are so poor, we humans, at understanding the best timing of things."

"I suppose you are right. Oh, I almost had that kitten in my arms. I could just spit with frustration."

Sunshine laughed and tussled my hair. Changing the subject, she said, "Tomorrow is your day of service, Whippoorwill. I know you will enjoy that."

"Yes, I do look forward to that. I get to see everyone first thing in the morning, don't I? Oh, but isn't tomorrow my last day?" I said, returning to my fretful mood.

"Yes, it is. But the good news is that we will be leaving at the same time as you, Mayan and me. And I believe that Keeya is on the same schedule as well. We will ride together to the train. Train together to the town. That will be fun."

"Well, I am certainly glad of that, but not so glad to be leaving. There is so much that I still don't understand about this place."

"Tell me some of your questions."

"How could Pearl be the donkey that I knew in the park, and yet younger and perfectly healthy?"

"I can't answer that question, I'm afraid. Humphry would say that there are some things we won't ever understand about the mystery of this place. I presume we are given to understand what we can, and we must leave the rest to be revealed someday."

"I suppose it's best to look at it that way. But not having answers only makes me think of more questions. For instance, is Rembrandt the same owl from the vision we had together?" This was the first time I had mentioned this shared vision since we had both experienced it on our first day together. Sunshine smiled, looking over at the owl.

"Yes, he is. I gave him the name Rembrandt when I arrived here, though he is a wild creature and of course had no previous name, as Pearl did. Pearl was named by a favorite handler at the park. Did you know? This man knew how precious she was."

"I didn't know that. Oh, she is precious, that much is certain," I agreed, scratching the donkey at the base of her great ears. "But how do you know this?"

"Mayan sees things and tells me some of what he sees."

"Does Mayan have some sort of grand destiny, do you think? Will he be very well known around the globe? I wouldn't be surprised if he was going to bring peace to the world and save us all."

"I'm not so sure that the answers to those questions can be the same," Sunshine said, lost for a moment in thought. "I suspect that those who are truly saving the world, as you put it, those who are bringing peace, are not the ones known around the globe. They work in humble ways; they are the quiet ones doing small tasks."

"But don't they need to be in a position of power to effect the world?"

"I used to believe that, but I've come to question it."

"Then what lies behind these quiet people's power?"

"Love," answered Sunshine.

"But anyone can love. Even I can do that."

"Exactly."

"But I don't see how love can save the world. How does it operate?"

"It extends—it is always extending. One heart loving another and another and another."

"But what if it bumps up against hate?"

"Oh, but love is the only power that has a chance against hate. Its warmth is capable of melting the crust of hatred."

"But don't you need some sort of platform? Some way of getting into the public eye to have this kind of overreaching effect?"

"On the contrary. I suspect fame and power are more of a hindrance to the extension of love, than an advantage. Think of it. If you met a powerful, famous person, would you be yourself around them?"

"Probably not. I would be all goofy and tongue-tied."

"And if you were in need of loving comfort, who would you run to?"

"Someone who loved me. My mother, a friend."

"Isn't it funny how we fantasize about becoming famous and powerful, and it's possibly the worst thing that can happen to us? No one would be themselves in our presence, and no one would come to us for comfort."

It was then that Sunshine spoke of her late husband. "Mayan's father was a professor at a university. He was a good deal older than I. He taught something called comparative religion and was a good teacher. His students were quite fond of him. Over the years he developed a reputation, and students came from all over Asia to study with him. These were young people, looking for spiritual direction. Some of them grew to almost worship my husband, and he felt very uncomfortable with this attention. He used to tell me that it was impossible to teach someone who saw their teacher as a sort of celebrity. It was an unhealthy relationship. 'Everyone is the same size, Sunshine,' he would say to me. 'Everyone is exactly the same size.' These students of his could no longer see my husband's humanity. He was almost a god to them."

And then, speaking of the vision we had shared together over the funeral scene in India, Sunshine continued. "The young man who you saw, the one at the edge of the crowd, was a friend, a true friend, and someone my husband could depend on to see as his equal. However learned this man believed my husband to be, he knew that he was just a man, just a man who had studied and could impart knowledge. They had wonderful talks together."

"He was so full of sadness for you and Mayan," I interjected.

"Yes." Sunshine looked out over the lake, thoughtful, slightly pained.

"When Rembrandt appeared and hovered over me and Mayan at my husband's burial, his crowd of adorers all came to the same conclusion: that this was my husband's spirit come to claim me and Mayan as his to protect, his to keep, forever. Have you ever known a crowd of people who agreed to think the same thing, Whippoorwill? This can be quite beautiful or quite unhealthy. It can lead to good or very bad consequences."

"I think I have, yes. Sometimes my classmates in school will suddenly turn on someone, usually another kid in the class, and everyone joins in. It feels a little sickening."

She looked at me. "Precisely. And feeling a bit sickened is often the first warning sign. We must pay attention to these feelings. You are wise to see this at your age. Try to keep your thoughts purely yours so that they never become poisoned by a group of people determined to believe the same thing, especially if you sense that belief to be unhealthy."

"I promise," I said to her. "And were you sickened that day from the group's thoughts?"

"These thoughts clung to me, they bound me. His admirers would continue to visit, telling me how blessed I was to be his, my husband's beloved, to be his entirely. They envied me this, and I felt rather ungrateful when I secretly wished to be my own, or God's, or simply a member of the family of man. I lived like this for over five years."

"I'm so sorry, Sunshine."

"The vision that we saw of the funeral, the knowledge that the appearance of the owl was meant to be a comfort, and not a life sentence, was utterly liberating. I am free now."

"I could tell this when I saw you that evening. And there's more, isn't there?"

"Yes, there's more." She smiled at my knowing. "He is a very good man. He loves Mayan, and Mayan loves him."

"Yes, Mayan told me so."

"That is sweet for me to hear," Sunshine said, smiling.

"Will I see you and Mayan again? Do you think?" I asked her.

"Mayan tells me so. Your work will have you traveling."

"My work…" I said, dreamily. "That makes leaving this place a little easier."

We sat together for a while, eating our sandwiches, watching the lake. The kitten did not return.

"Percival is organizing a bonfire for tonight," Sunshine said. "Had you heard?"

"No. What fun. Does he need help?"

"He could use some, I think. Though Mary is willing to gather wood, her tendency leans a bit too much toward the massive. I believe Cowslip should be here soon, and we can ride back together."

At which point Cowslip magically appeared, moving down the path toward us.

"And that is another thing," I said to Sunshine. "How is it that the timing of the appearance of people and animals that one needs is so spot-on in this place, as if anticipated?"

"I think you answered the question yourself,

Whippoorwill, with the word *anticipated*. Perhaps we are easier to read than we think. Perhaps anticipating our needs is a simpler equation than it appears. Perhaps the Bright Ones are closer to us here."

"A gathering place, maybe?" I offered. "Where a choir of spirits can come to meet from all over: all over the world, all over the animal kingdom, and, most importantly, all over time. A place where there is no separation of beings that are joined together by love. And that is why we can be with those who have crossed over and into the next world. We still love them, so they are still with us."

"You understand now, Whippoorwill, the great power of love."

"Hmm…" I answered, and then added, "Oooooo, I could love that little kitten. I sure could love that little darling kitten."

14

"Oh, but I had already given a name to the kitten, you see," I said to George as we gathered wood together for the bonfire. "Maybe that's why I am sick over coming so close to catching her and then losing her."

"And what name have you given her, Whippoorwill?" George asked.

"Daffodil. She's yellow and reminds me of springtime and rebirth and happiness."

"That's a fine name."

"Do you think I will see her again? Do you think this story will end happily?"

"It wouldn't be much of a story, would it," answered George, "if we knew the ending before we were told the tale? We would miss all of its goodness."

"Oh, sometimes I can be such an eleven-year-old!" I groaned. "I've been a horrid little pill today. And so much good has happened, so much miraculous good! I'm such an ingrate!" I bellowed, grabbing my head.

George had a good laugh over this last line.

Watching his good face light up with humor caused me to continue with a lighter heart. "I know that you believe in many beautiful things, George. I feel as if you, of all people, might have the power to help me to believe in beautiful things too. And I imagine that if I were able to believe in all of the beautiful things that you believe, I might find my way to trusting in these beautiful things and not falling into doubt every three minutes."

George took a moment to think before he responded. "Doubts, uncertainties are what we first see when we look into the unknown."

"Then they are natural, expected?" I asked. "But some of mine are so mean that they squash everything in their path. How will I know whether a thought, an idea such as the one I received this morning about my calling to play a role in the healing of the planet is true or false?"

George took another moment to study me. "Truth is a living thing, Whippoorwill. Does the idea stir the life inside of you?"

"I believe so. Yes. But what I don't understand is, why was I born on the paved and concrete island of Manhattan? Isn't this an odd beginning for a life in the study of nature?"

"If you follow your story closely and take time to reflect, someday there might come a moment when you can see the wisdom behind the pattern, and all will come clear, or some of the pattern, I should say. The pattern can be intricate and quite complex. You might be able to see how the gifts given to you and the choices you made around these gifts created a path."

"But will the story be right?"

"If your story has love in it, if it has passion, beauty, patience, hope, caring, kindness, any of these, it will have been a life worth living. All lives are worth living because they can always lead us to love."

I took a big sigh. "Oh, how I could love that little Daffodil."

George had another big laugh, and this time I joined him.

It was Percival's voice that cut through our reverie, calling us to gather around the constructed bonfire to view our work. The pile of wood was a grand spectacle, made especially formidable by the addition of an enormous, fallen tree that Mary had dragged out of the woods. It looked as if a family of giants had visited to help with our effort. We stood back to marvel at our creation.

When I returned to my little cabin for my bath, it occurred to me that I had not seen Sebastian since I left him in the morning. I tried to remember whether I had noticed him while the group had gathered wood for the fire. No, I thought, he wasn't there. I had grown used to having Sebastian watching over me. He slept by the fire in the sitting room every night, which was a comfort to me. I understood that Sebastian was more of a free agent, that unlike Pearl, he was part of the system of this place. He was the courier, and perhaps the protector of those my age, who arrived at the Mother Lake unaccompanied by an adult. I didn't feel I needed his protection now, but I missed him and wondered what might have taken him away. I would have to ask my friends at the evening meal if any of them had seen him.

That evening our choir went directly to its meal and saved its singing for the bonfire, where all of us gathered, all of the humans and animals and horses. Even some of the wild forest animals, drawn by our revelry, peeked around trees and bushes to watch us. I distinctly recognized the fox we had passed on our journey from the train. All of us, with the exception of Sebastian, I noted, were in attendance. It seemed no one had seen him throughout the day. Though Mayan, I could see, was not the least bit concerned. It's wonderful how one person being unworried can calm the worry of another. Mayan often filled this role, as of course did George.

The blaze that night from our fire might have reached the notice of the moon. Our voices in song might have kept the trees awake, shaken the sleepy flowers out of their slumber. Keeya and Estrellita danced the elegant dances from their fatherlands, and we all followed in their footsteps, mimicking their understated, simple steps. We sang and sang and sang some more. We even sang Percival's schoolmate's song about warts. Mayan taught us a song about the wisdom of worms. And finally, I taught them all the song that I used to sing to Pearl. And, when we sang it together, Pearl lost all gravity. Kicking up her heels, she brayed and began to run in large circles around and around the humans who stood by the fire.

I wonder, dear reader, whether you have ever had the privilege of attending a city dog run. We had one very near where we lived in Manhattan, and my mother and I would go in the late afternoons for the after work dog romp show. This is when the people returned home and brought their dogs to the enclosed run to play. There was always one dog, sometimes an unlikely choice, such as a short-legged dachshund, that would enter the dog run, and once released from its leash, would proceed to make one joyful lap around the inside of the enclosure. This simple movement would for some reason stir up every last dog in the run for a chase. And though it is a fact that most dogs will prefer their role of either chaser or chasee, every dog in the run would be willing to throw all of their notions of their preferred roles to chase this one dog. Around and around and around they would go, at full-out mad-racing speed, helpless against the pull to chase. Eventually, the owner of the starter dog would call her canine friend to her side, and all of the dogs would stop, tongues hanging out, and attempt to return to their senses.

Pearl was the instigator that evening, and all the animals—horses, otter, antelope, sheep, leopard, owl, and finally elephant—lost all decorum and chased, and then chased some more, and chased yet again my mad-glad donkey around and around and around the perimeter of our gathering. The ground shook with beating hooves and pads and paws, as we humans turned and turned watching the ecstasy of the chase. Finally, I called to Pearl, and she trotted over to me. This in turn caused all of the animals to slow their pace and eventually come to a panting stop.

Mary was the first to fold herself near to the fire and begin to grow sleepy. After some time she lay herself full-out on the ground and fell heavily asleep, inspiring all of the diurnal animals (I know what that means now) to snuggle in near to her. After which she set up a great, rumbling, deep intake breathing pattern which allowed us to be a special club of those who have witnessed a snoring elephant.

That night we were so engaged in our night's merriments that we did not notice the approach of a figure who stood at the edge of the circle, presumably observing our enjoyment. Another, smaller figure stood next to him in silence. The smaller of the figures, impatient for our attention, finally barked. We all turned.

"Humphry!" Sunshine exclaimed.

"And Sebastian!" I added, relieved.

All of us leapt to our feet, circling them, and asking questions.

"How long have you been standing there?" asked Percival.

"Have you come from the town?" Estrellita wondered.

"Did Sebastian meet you at the train?" I questioned.

"Did you come by horse?" Sunshine wanted to know, turning to count the number of horses in the herd. "And have you eaten?" she added.

"Monkshood carried me from the train and my good Sebastian came to meet me. We were fol-lowed by a rather flighty herd of mountain cattle. I have indulged in a long dowsing in the waters of the Mother Lake and have found sufficient sustenance from the kitchen for both Sebastian and me." He smiled at us all, as a proud father might seeing all of his good children together enjoying themselves. "I trust that you have all fallen thoroughly in love with one another, and now understand a little of the magic of this place, which understanding has, of course, led to even more questions." Humphry paused to smile, taking us all in. "I presume George has had time to talk to each of you, and by now you know who each of your brother and sister animal companions are to you. I hope you have all had your time on the island of memories and have enjoyed long and healing swims in the waters of the Mother." After a moment he added, "I hope I am not too late to join the choir."

To say that we took up our singing and that we sang all night would be a slight exaggeration. It felt as if we might have done so to me. At one point Keeya and I stood to either side of Humphry and asked our burning questions about our parents.

"Have you seen my mother, Humphry, in her retreat place?" I asked, eagerly.

Humphry made a very poor attempt at hiding his delight. "I might have done so, yes."

"And have you seen my father? And are they all

googly-eyed over one another?" asked Keeya, with an impish grin.

"They do seem a bit glazed," Humphry confessed.

"And was this somehow part of the plan?" I asked, "getting those two together without the two of us around, possibly messing things up?"

"I am just a cog, my dears, a cog in the wheel of fate." He grinned.

"Will we ever have all of our questions answered about this place, about this week?" I added.

"It depends on what you mean by answers," Humphry replied rather vaguely.

"I mean about the Mother Lake, the Bright Ones, the animal companions, I mean about everything," I blurted.

It was at this point that I felt the small body of a giggling child next to me and realized that Mayan had crept into our circle to have a little fit of laughter.

"Mayan, my friend," said Humphry, "have you discovered all of the answers that Whippoorwill is seeking?"

"No, I've found something even better,"

answered Mayan, through his chortling. "I've discovered belly-aching comedy."

"And where did you discover this?" asked
Humphry.

"Lunch Box," answered Mayan.

"And what will you do with this discovery?"

"Bring it back to India with me. Share it with
Uncle Bookshop," he said, beaming. "Did you know
that a good laughing fit can stretch your insides so
that you can fit that much more happiness inside
of you?"

"No," said Keeya and I almost at the same time.

"Fact," assured Mayan, "clean fact."

This made all three of us laugh.

All the while Sebastian remained glued to
Humphry's side, often looking over and into his
face like a child into his mother's eyes. This was
the moment when I understood that Sebastian
was Humphry's dog, his special companion. I
understood that I would be heading back to my
cabin with my beautiful Pearl as my guardian, and
that Sebastian would be with his human friend for
the night.

Eventually all of us made the decision to go off

to our beds. The animals stood and stretched, the humans stood and stretched, and Rembrandt stretched and flapped his wings before flying off to explore the night. Pearl found me in the waning firelight, and we took the path together to our cabin. She would stay outside, I presumed, as she always preferred, and I would learn to sleep alone in my cabin, which had become as dear to me as my bedroom at home. I would miss watching Sebastian curl up in front of the fire but was happy for him that he was reunited with his human.

"Pearl," I said to my pointy-eared, patient friend. "If what I understand to be true about our animal friends and our need of the qualities that they exhibited to us during our time with them, then I must be in need of patience." We walked on in silence. But, as I might have mentioned before, perhaps seventy-seven times by now, I am never silent for long. "So I must assume that in the case of my coming to understand all of the workings of the Bright Ones, all the miracles behind the journey of a lifetime, that eventually, one secret at a time, the truth behind this pattern will be revealed, and that it is up to me to live my life to its fullest, and to try and practice patience."

We were in front of the cabin when Pearl moved around in front of me and stopped me for a moment before I entered. She placed her dear, round, black nose on my heart and held it there. "Thank you, my good angel," I answered, kissing her on her head. "I'll see you in the morning." And we went off to our beds.

I could never understand why there was always a fire burning in the fireplace in the little sitting room of my cabin. I had never seen anyone attend to it. Sebastian had slept beside it for warmth every night, but I had no idea how it had remained lit and warm.

It was the only light in the cabin that night, making the sitting room seem even cozier, if that were possible. It was quite late, and I thought I should get into bed without stopping to warm myself at the fire, as I was to be in service the next morning and would need my sleep.

Stepping into my bedroom, I froze, utterly shocked. Too overwhelmed to scream, I let out a sort of half mumbled squeal which, had the cabins been nearer to one another, might have been heard by everyone in the camp. I stood gaping and sputtering. There was something on my bed. Eventually I found my words.

"You are not as large as a bread box," I whispered, "but I think I know who sent you to me."

15

DAFFODIL TOOK turns sleeping on my stomach, my legs, and my head all night. Just before dawn she stirred and made the first sound I had heard from her, a sweet mewing, which turned into a robust purr as I reached to pet her. I was delighted by the early hour as it meant that I could play with Daffodil for a time before I had to dash to the kitchen for the preparation of breakfast. Looking around for something to entertain my kitten, I discovered that I needn't have bothered for everything was entertaining to Daffodil. We went out in the garden to play as the sun began to make its suggested appearance. I felt that there was no better time to practice trust than the present. I trusted that once connected to me, Daffodil would not run away, and I was proven right. Pearl had slept in the garden that night and, due to her late-night revelry, continued with her deep slumber while Daffodil and I explored. Exploring a garden with a kitten is very different than exploring a garden with a human. I was on my belly most of the time, watching as Daffodil interacted with the plants. She viewed the half-waking flowers with slow creeping wonder.

Respectful, for the most part, she sniffed, occasionally batted, and sometimes sat staring at the plant beings around her. I use the term being because she so clearly communicated with the individual inhabitants of the garden as if they were as animate as she. On occasion, she would simply stand next to a plant and still herself, as if listening, and after a moment turn to face the green, growing thing in recognition of its slow communications. I could see that morning that Daffodil was destined to teach me something about how to understand plant life, a skill which would serve me a lifetime along my chosen path, which had everything to do, I suspected that morning, with slowing and listening. This suspicion has since proven its worth.

I don't wish to imply that Daffodil was always slow and thoughtful. She would occasionally leap into the air and go tearing off in all directions as if being chased, and then come tearing back to me, once landing with perfect precision on my shoulder. Several times, she skittered over Pearl's recumbent body, causing Pearl to groan lazily, open her eyes and close them, ever patient with young ones. We played like this for a good hour before Daffodil's eyelids grew heavy, and she tucked herself up against the side of Pearl's great head and fell deeply asleep. The image of my two dear ones asleep next to one another will always cause me to smile.

Free to begin my day of service, I ran all the way to the kitchen and burst through the door to find Percival humming happily as he prepared food.

"I hope I am not late," I apologized. "I've been having the most yippee-skippee morning!"

"That wouldn't be caused by a tiny, yellow, mewing creature named after a spring flower of the same color, would it?"

"Why does everyone seem to know every good thing about me before I learn it?"

"It's easier to see some things from a slight distance."

"What do you mean?"

"Have you noticed how much easier it is to see another's faults? Say, a friend's? And how difficult it is to see your own?"

"Like gossiping? Yes."

"And have you noticed how much easier it is to see another's strengths than it is to see your own?"

"I am beginning to see this, yes, like the qualities that we all share with our special animals. I can see Mayan's rare uniqueness, Sunshine's loyalty, Keeya's combination of strength and gentleness, Estrellita's joy of the natural world." And I almost added, but didn't want to embarrass him, Percival's great big, warm-hearted generosity.

"You see the point precisely," Percival assured me.

"And yet, I cannot see my own patience. I am most impatient."

"But that is the beginning of taking on any admirable quality: the challenge of its opposite.

True patience will grow out of a desire to tame impatience."

"I think I am able to understand that."

"Just as true generosity of spirit comes from the desire to tame a tendency to be stingy."

"Are you talking about anyone in particular?" I asked.

Percival smiled and explained, "I was always unwilling as a kid to share my father with anyone else. He was mine, I believed, all mine. The problem was, he was a politician. He belonged to a great number of people, or so he believed, and still believes. And a great number of people belong to him, or so many of them believe, as he believes."

"When did you begin to grow large hearted?"

"I think it was when I spent my week with Mary and observed her in her role as the matriarch of a herd of elephants. She took me into her herd as well. It was the beginning of the easing of my tight grip on my father. I could understand that some people are suited for this role in society and that my father had a true gift as a leader. It's been twenty years now since that time and I have made a bit of progress."

"Oh, I should say so, Percival. You are the

biggest-hearted person I have ever met. There, I said it."

Percival's face went limp with wonder, and he looked inside of himself for a moment, as many of us will do when we receive a true compliment—not an ingenuine one, but a genuine one. He thought for a moment and smiled at me.

"That's the nicest thing anyone has ever said to me, Whippoorwill."

"I meant it," I assured him.

I have thought often of this simple exchange with Percival over the years, and whenever I do, I am reminded never to hold back a true compliment. Most people cannot see their truest gifts, like Percival and his generosity of spirit. Some of us will hold back a compliment because we are shy, or don't want to appear to be too syrupy. But a true compliment, one that is simply identifying a lovable quality that we can see shining through the other, can never be construed as false flattery. A true compliment holds the power to allow a little more light to shine through the gift and out into the world.

Changing the subject, Percival offered, "I have

a present for you from all of us. We've been up to some arts and crafts while you weren't looking." And at that, he pulled out from behind a counter the most darling contraption. Made of light wood with a sort of twiggy netting, it looked like something that an elf would choose to live in, with the softest mossy padding on its floor.

I stared at it for a time and then understood. "It's a travel carrying case for my kitten! Oh, I love it!" I hollered and hugged it to my chest. "I love, love, love it!" I bellowed some more and danced around the kitchen with my gift. "I adore the dandy little thing!"

"Are you two ever going to bring me some breakfast?" we heard from outside the door. Humphry's good face appeared, beaming with pleasure. "I've come to be of some assistance," he continued. "I couldn't sleep in, as everyone else must be able to do this morning." And then turning to me he asked, "How is our little Daffodil this morning?"

"But how is it that everyone, everyone around here, knew of my little Daffodil before I did?" I asked.

"It is mysterious, isn't it?" agreed Humphry.

"The lake is full of such mysteries," echoed Percival.

"Ohhhhh," I wailed in mock frustration. "If anything was sent to me to strengthen my patience it's those two comments!" I grabbed my hair, pulling it out to the sides of my head. "But I want to know everything! EVERYTHING about this MYSTERY!"

"Are we ever going to rustle up some breakfast?" asked Humphry, pouring himself a cup of coffee, which Percival had steaming on the stove.

"Is that coffee I smell?" said a voice outside the door before Sunshine's face popped into view.

"Is there anything a six-year-old might eat?" added Mayan, following his mother through the door with his beautiful leopard. "Ruby tells me that I must eat more, especially if I am to be expected to sing all night."

Keeya's antelope was the next head to pop through the door, with Keeya, breathless on her heels, clearly already having had a fine run through the forest. "Could I get everyone some juice?" She moved into the kitchen in search of something to drink.

Estrellita was the next to arrive, dripping from head to toe having had an early morning swim in the Mother Lake, her water-slick otter slipping in beside her.

"It's time for a breakfast party, I see," announced Percival.

"But what about George? Shall I run and wake him?" I offered.

"Oh, George popped off after last night's revelries," said Humphry.

"In the middle of the night? But how did he get to the train?" I asked. And at this everyone smiled. I waited for some sort of explanation.

Humphry took the challenge. "George doesn't need a train to go where he is headed."

"Oh," I sighed. "More mystery!"

We had our breakfast next to the Mother Lake, humans and animals, munching, chatting, happy as a litter of kit foxes.

"Oh, I'm going to miss you all so much," I lamented.

"It has been sweet, all of us together in one place," Sunshine agreed.

"Maybe we should plan a reunion?" I suggested.

Everyone chuckled quietly at this.

"Why do you all look as if you are in on a joke, and I am the only clueless one?"

It was Sunshine who came to my rescue. "We're smiling because now that we have been brought together, there is little hope of our shaking one another. We are meant to walk this world together, and the next, I presume."

"More mystery for Whippoorwill! Is that what mysticism means? Is that the definition of the mystical? Hm? Things that poor Whippoorwill doesn't quite understand?"

It was Mayan who chimed in next. "You understand more than you think. Have you ever said of something that you have just pronounced, something that might have been questioned by someone with a 'How do you know that?' Have you ever answered with a 'I just know'?"

"Yes," I responded.

Keeya chimed in next. "Maybe that's the definition of the mystical. Maybe some knowledge is a kind of knowing that you can't prove. Like who you love, for instance, or better yet, who you trust."

"George spoke about our handful, as he called them," I added. "Those who we are meant to have in our lives. So it's love that brings us together?"

"That, yes," Sunshine interjected, "but I would guess that it's trust that will keep us together. It was George who wrote, 'To be trusted is a greater compliment than to be loved.'"

"Isn't that the same thing?" I asked.

"You can love someone who you don't trust. A parent can love an untrustworthy child, for instance," explained Sunshine.

"I would certainly trust George to know most things," said Keeya.

"He talked to me about having some sort of compass inside of me that will guide me," I offered.

"He told me that I had found my life's work," said Estrellita.

"He told me that I would follow in his foot-steps," Percival shared, a little shyly, "that I was to write something that would have an effect on many people."

"Oh my," exclaimed Sunshine. "What a blessing."

"I told him that he must have the wrong Percival, that I wasn't a writer."

"And what did he say to that?" I asked.

"First, he asked me, 'Do you read?' I told him that indeed I did read, I loved to read. and he smiled and said, 'The art of writing is a shy beast; it often won't appear until one has something to say.'"

"'But I haven't been to school for writing,'" I argued, 'and I'm almost thirty years old.' He chuckled at this. 'But you read?' he repeated. 'Well…' I began to explain, and he stopped me."

"Oh, you are speaking of style and grammar, two rather fickle characters. Don't worry, the inspiration will drive the effort, and the Bright Ones will bring you the right aid."

"You're speaking of an editor, I hope."

"That and others."

It turns out each of us had had our special talk with George. Keeya would follow in Estrellita's footsteps, as would I, with all of us working in the field of preservation and restoration of the natural world. And we would be a part of a much greater network of souls destined to bring the world back into health. We were assured that any help needed along this path would arrive when we needed it. I wondered most about what it was Mayan was to accomplish in this life. Of all of us, Mayan seemed most destined to greatness.

"Mayan, can you share what George said to you? I imagine you are destined to do something grand." I felt this must be true, though I wondered whether his destiny might be something that shouldn't be exposed too early, that perhaps his greatness needed to be hidden for a while until it was ready to surprise the world.

Mayan laughed to himself. "I don't want to disappoint you, Whippoorwill, but my role on the world's stage will be barely a noticeable one. When I asked what I was meant to do with this life, he answered, 'There are some souls whose worth is only counted where the Bright Ones live. These souls will not perform a worldly function so much as love the performance of the world. Their calling is to see the truth behind the workings of the world, which is love. Their work is to love…'"

All of us were quiet as we attempted to take this in. "I know. It isn't very majestic, is it?" Mayan added, "But George assures me that it is of great importance to the world. That love feeds everything on the earth, that the planet and its beings would die without it. That the world would actually starve to death without our love. When George told me this, I felt like the luckiest goose in the big world of geese." Mayan continued, "I felt like I had been given the greatest duty of them all, greater than any president, leader, king, emperor. I felt like I had been given a superpower."

"I can't think of a better job for you, Mayan," Estrellita responded.

"Nor can I," echoed Sunshine, with everyone chiming in.

It was at this point that Percival suggested we go sailing. "The little rowboats have sails, did you know? The wind is up, it might be fun."

"But I don't know how to sail," said Estrellita.

"Neither do I," added Keeya.

"Me neither," said Sunshine.

"I don't have a clue," I said, with Mayan agreeing and completing the circle.

"Well, to be perfectly honest, I don't know how to sail either," Percival confessed, "but how difficult could it be? I am thinking that the wind and the Mother will teach us."

We'd all grown accustomed to trusting that the great Mother Lake would have the answers, believing so thoroughly in her powers that we hopped up from our seats on the ground as a group and skipped to the shore to choose our vessels, with Sunshine and Mayan taking one boat and the rest of us choosing one of our own. After we had secured our mast and raised our sails, we took off in our various, mad-shifting, tipsy directions.

With none of us having any idea what we were doing, we careened around, nearly crashing into one another, almost tipping over, throwing our weight around. Our little crafts dashed forward, stood still, traveled sideways, and threatened to pitch over entirely. I distinctly observed Percival, at one point, traveling backward.

To say that the wind was playful that morning would be an understatement. Seeming to change directions constantly, it was as fickle as the flight of a hummingbird. We were tossed around by fits and starts for quite a while before one of us, I believe it was me, decided that it would be fun to try and race one another.

"Race you to the shore," I yelled out to Keeya, as I attempted to catch a gust of wind that I guessed might blow me in that general direction. My little sail tipped and flapped, lost all wind, then puffed up violently. Keeya wrestled with her boat to meet the challenge.

"Last one there is a big loser!" I added, when *plop!* over I went into the water, boat upside down, with me wheezing, scrambling, bouncing in the water, and finally laughing so hard I almost choked.

Keeya turned to see my predicament, doubled over laughing, and finally, turning to Percival, yelled, "One down and the rest to go. First one there is the biggest winner of them all!" And *plop!* over went Keeya into the drink, gulping, splashing, laughing with her little boat upside down.

Percival was next, though he seemed to have taken on the role of worst sailor ever, turning his tiny craft around and heading for the shore. "Move over, you land-loving amateurs, and watch a real pro. First one there is a rock star!" And *plop!* over Percival toppled, in a grand display of awkwardness. It was an arm-flailing, leg-flying, cannonball-splashing event, leading to the three of us attempting to right our little boats. We did so by crawling up the sides of the slick bottoms of our up-sided boats; inching ourselves toward the rudder before we lost all traction and swiftly slid back into the water; pulling up and sliding back, pulling and sliding; always laughing, which made it hard to do anything but just lie back in the water and laugh.

Estrellita was next to attempt to join in our race. "Last one there is a sad sack of a ruin. I'm going to

be queen of the shore, the biggest winner ever!"
And over she went. More graceful than Percival,
but swimming now, boat upside down, laughing
and scrambling to right her boat.

It was then that we all looked over at the utterly
peaceful and skillful Mayan, gracefully guiding
his little vessel with his mother sitting restfully
aboard, smiling, gliding, traveling where the wind
wished them to go, their craft moving like a swan,
evenly balanced between the tension of movement
and wind.

When I say we all turned to look at them, I
include here the animals. For it seemed that all
the animals had stayed behind on the shore, lined
up, side by side to study the behavior of their
humans.

I imagine in some ways they saw us as being
quite a bit like they had been as young animals,
playing for the sake of playing. Pretending to com-
pete. Chasing one another around. All animals will
play. They will especially play in the springtime,
when the seriousness of making it through the win-
ter is past, and they have enough food in their bellies to spend a little energy running around after
one another simply for the joy of it.

I'm not sure which one of our animals broke the spell, but in an instant, they were all in the water, swimming out to play with us.

I have since thought of this day and how curative a rousing playdate can be. And how very different in tone is a true act of play from that which involves competition. Of course, I should have realized that the Mother Lake would never allow a contest in her waters, even if entered into in jest. I should have known that the minute one of us expressed a desire to win, to beat another in contest, the minute I challenged Keeya to a race, the Mother had to tip me over, she had to, and so on through our little group of competitors. That our laughter sprung from this understanding was clear. How lovely to be somewhere where rivalry was not allowed, and more delicious, where it seemed absurd. This caused us to laugh all the harder.

Animals play when they play—there is no gray area. Humans will believe that they are playing a game of tennis, for instance, when too often, I'm afraid, there isn't the slightest sense of play in them. The same goes for many sports. We participate in a sport; we don't always play at a sport.

That day, having been so comically pitched

overboard, we humans began to play in earnest. And when the animals could see that we had entered into a true frolic, they all joined us, all of them: elephant, leopard, donkey, antelope, otter, and owl. Mary helped to right our little boats with her great trunk, allowing us to climb back aboard, where we continued to exhibit our pathetic sailing skills. We played at pirates, marauding each other's boats, and tossing one another overboard. This made room for others, sometimes one of the animals, to try their skills at sailing. I know that I saw the giant otter attempting to sail Percival's boat, which effort turned out to be about as successful as Percival's attempts. And through this joyous game of ours of getting nowhere sailed the placid mother and son, laughing, gracefully gliding through the water with Rembrandt circling serenely above.

Of course, we turned on them, of course we did. We all did, even the animals. We had to upend them. We dove, crawled, paddled, and half-sailed to position ourselves in a wide circle around the graceful duo in their confident little vessel.

"I'm afraid we've been found out, Mayan," remarked Sunshine. "They're coming for us."

Mayan cackled and came about, and about again, and about once more, escaping our attempts at ambush at every turn. We simply had to take them.

"You'll never escape us!" yelled Estrellita.

"We have you surrounded!" added Percival.

"Should we wave the white flag, Mayan?" asked Sunshine.

"Never!" whispered Mayan, placidly skimming through the gaps in our circle.

It was Estrellita's giant otter that finally caught up with the little boat. He climbed aboard, took an assessment of the two peaceful voyagers, and crawled into Sunshine's lap, as if it had just occurred to the otter that he required a nap. This allowed the little craft to slip through our circle and head for the shore in safety.

"Turncoat!" yelled Percival, and wrestled with his sail, setting out for the chase. We never caught them.

That day ruined us all, forever, for any sort of competition. We will play games, especially when we get together, but never will we keep score. And if one of us is in danger of winning, we will announce that the purpose of the game was in fact to lose, and therefore the winner is the biggest loser of them all.

So far, this attitude has served me very well. At the end of my long life I hope to have collected no signs of being a winner: awards, trophies, keys to cities, unwarranted degrees. The only degree I hope to be known for is the degree of delight that I took in the world.

16

AFTER OUR long play we each walked off to our various cabins. Pearl and I wandered slowly back to our little Daffodil. She was wide awake now and chasing bugs, leaping and darting about the garden. I showed her the traveling basket that had been made for her, and she happily climbed in for an exploration, found it to her liking, settled in, and began to groom herself for her future travels. Pearl fell into a deep and well-deserved sleep on a mossy bed next to the garden.

That evening, while soaking in my mother's water bath, Daffodil sat on the windowsill above and studied me as only a cat will do. She was as still as a photograph, eyes focused, with a look of unbreakable interest. I would swear that she was reading the story of my life to date, and furthermore, she was assessing how she was to fit into its future.

Have you ever, dear reader, experienced a moment in your life where another, a human or an animal, suddenly makes perfect sense in your life? It is as if you had found an important piece of a jigsaw puzzle, and snuggled it inside its cavity, and the whole picture comes into focus. Daffodil fit. She fit me perfectly, this much was clear. And during that intense session of study, Daffodil was learning, I presume, that I was a perfect fit for her as well.

Daffodil is still with me as I write this, sitting beside me in her mature glory, as I enter the seventh year of third decade on the planet. She has traveled with me back and forth to Africa, loved me through my teenage years, seen me through most of my twenties. She remains a delightful constant in my life. I understand that she will someday join Tinker in the next world to await my arrival, which will hopefully not occur for many more years. I presume that both of my dear kitty friends will be watched over by a very patient donkey.

My mother took instantly to Daffodil, allowing her to nest on occasion in her lovely hair. There have been times, when at school, or traveling to India or Peru, where I have left Daffodil with Louise, whether with our family in Botswana or our visits to Manhattan, and Daffodil has never been anything but content with this arrangement.

Pearl, by the way, has made regular visits to my dream world over the years. When she does show up in a dream, she always brings with her the gift of her patience. These dreams are quite ordinary, not the fantastic, changeable types of dreams, but the quiet, thoughtful ones with just the two of us sitting with one another and talking. She doesn't so much talk, but she manages to convey to me what she thinks, and her thinking is always something that shows me the way to walk through any difficulty I might be experiencing with just a little more patience than that which I believed myself capable. She reminds me that there is a time for all ideas to come to fruition, that I must wait for the seed to be planted, watered, fertilized, given time to sprout and bud, and finally fruit. This is very helpful advice when you are working to save a planet. All good ideas will come to maturity, she assures me, all will ripen and be harvested.

One tradition that our group from the Mother Lake has initiated is a once-weekly circle of concern for our beautiful planet. We gather, all of us, no matter where we are around the world, to focus our love on our Mother Earth. Mayan is the one to call us together, a call we each receive through our thoughts. The appeal is unmistakable as Mayan's thoughts are filled with light—he is our beacon. When this occurs, each of us will experience a little shower of sparkly lights in our mind's eye, which will signal that it is time to step away for a moment from what we are doing and to send out our small lights of hope around the earth. We could be in the middle of the woods or in the middle of London, the call could arrive in the middle of the day or the middle of the night, but each of us will stop what we are doing and imagine reaching out to hold one another's hands, as we encircle the Earth with our thoughts of love. Mayan assures us that this is having far-reaching, positive effects around the planet. Mayan never says anything merely to cheer us on, to shore us up, but he sees progress at a micro and macro level and assures us that these small thought efforts of healing are indeed affecting the balance of health for our dear Earth. This keeps Estrellita and Keeya and me going on those days when we are weary of the struggle in our chosen field. Of course, Sunshine and Percival benefit from his vision as well.

And speaking of Percival, he is writing a screenplay about the day the world wakes up. I am one of the handful who have read the manuscript. And I will say that I laughed until I was sick in some places and cried a bucket full of tears in others (healthy tears, tears of happiness). He tells me he's not sure of the manuscript. He tells me that he is not a writer. I ask him, "Then who is it that wrote this? That guy deserves a medal." I tell him about what Pearl confirms to me in my dreams, that there is a time for every good idea. I tell him that this project must and will come to full expression. I believe this with all my heart.

Estrellita encourages him—of course she does, she is a loving partner to Percival. I know, dear reader, I did not see this flowering either while we were in the mountains together. They took their time to give the little plant of their romance plenty of daylight to take root and thrive. It was Percival's father, the good politician, who campaigned the hardest for Estrellita to be Percival's bride. "You must marry that little star, Lunch Box, she will brighten your earthly days."

Sunshine wrote yesterday to say that Mayan has fallen in love, for the first and only time, he tells her. She believes him. Her own love has proven to be a great healing for her. She has not only blossomed in spirit but as an artist, an early passion of hers that was pushed to the back of the someday shelf when she married her first husband. she sends our human handful images of her drawings whenever we beg for her to share them. The drawings in this little book were rendered by Sunshine from her memory of our time in the mountains.

None of us has ever returned to Switzerland to go in search of our mountain sanctuary. It would seem disrespectful to visit without an invitation. I must assume that Humphry is still busily gathering handfuls of predestined friends together for their week in that magnificent place. This thought gives me hope for the world, the earth, the family of man, and the family of beasts.

I regularly call on the Bright Ones to help me. This habit will remain with me throughout my life, I am sure. I operate under the assumption that there is no distinguishing difference between the large and the small requests for aid. I will ask for their help in healing the planet as easily as a request for the healing of my little Daffodil.

As soon as I returned home, I visited our library to discover my first of George's books, *The Princess and the Goblin*, the story of a boy named Curdie and his escapades with the Princess Irene. I have gone on to read more and more of his books. There is always one of George's books next to my bed.

Oh, and wherever I find myself, I will find and join a choir. I have sung all over the world, never in any sort of grand, international chorus, but in small groups of individual voices, united in harmony, joining together for a bit of rejoicing. My favorite choir is the one that I share with my good sister Keeya, with its movement of understated footwork.

Before I leave you, dear reader, I will tell you a little about Mayan. He is now in his early twenties and hasn't lost an ounce of his joy for living. He still cackles when he laughs, still claps wildly when he is overjoyed, still sees and reports on the Bright Ones, still knows much more of the workings behind this life than the rest of us. And though I have visited India many times, I really needn't have bothered as Mayan does not need to be in my company to know all that goes on with his handful of people. A typical call from Mayan begins with a report of what he sees has been going on in my life, and a remedy for helping me through any sort of challenge.

I doubt that I will ever fully comprehend all the mystery that the Mother Lake held, but I often feel her continuing to teach me. Sometimes, when I come close to deeply loving someone, some creature, some forest or flower, I will feel her warm waters filling my chest with gladness, and I understand that I am a part of her, and she of me.

Margaret Dulaney has been writing essays on mystical themes for over a quarter of a century. In 2010 she began offering these writings on ListenWell.org, a website featuring once-monthly spoken word essays, exploring open-faith ideas through story and metaphor. She has authored three books: *To Hear the Forest Sing*, *The Parables of Sunlight* and *Spend Some Love*.

Margaret lives in Eastern Pennsylvania with her husband Matt Balitsaris in an old stone house filled with animal companions and surrounded by the company of long-loved trees. The elf hut above is tucked in the woods behind their home.

For more information visit: www.listenwell.org

www.ingramcontent.com/pod-product-compliance
Lightning Source LLC
Chambersburg PA
CBHW021413010826

48972CB00014B/1972